It was a spellbinding moment

''What would you do if I kissed you now?'' Sam asked playfully.

Kate gazed up into his dark blue eyes, her heart thudding in her chest. ''I don't suppose it would do much good to scream,'' she finally whispered.

He shook his head wisely, ''None at all.''

''Do the neighbors hear a lot of female screams coming from your place?''

''Only screams of delight,'' he murmured, lowering his mouth to hers. ''My advice is to cheerfully submit....''

THE AUTHOR

Jane Silverwood always wanted to be a writer. As a young girl, she tried her hand at short stories and novels. Real professional success came years later, after she left her teaching job to write full-time.

Slow Melt is Jane's second Temptation, although she's written several other books under various pseudonyms. A third Temptation is in the works, she reports.

Recent Books by Jane Silverwood

HARLEQUIN TEMPTATION
46—VOYAGE OF THE HEART

These books may be available at your local bookseller.

Don't miss any of our special offers. Write to us at the following address for information on our newest releases.

Harlequin Reader Service
901 Fuhrmann Blvd.,
P.O. Box 1325, Buffalo, N.Y. 14269
Canadian address: P.O. Box 2800, Postal Station A,
5170 Yonge St., Willowdale, Ont. M2N 6J3

Slow Melt

JANE SILVERWOOD

Harlequin Books

TORONTO • NEW YORK • LONDON
AMSTERDAM • PARIS • SYDNEY • HAMBURG
STOCKHOLM • ATHENS • TOKYO • MILAN

To Pat,
an inspiring skater

Published February 1986

ISBN 0-373-25193-9

SHE WAS GETTING too old for this, Kate thought. It was twenty minutes to eleven on an unseasonably chilly night early in November. As she pulled her Volkswagen bug into one of the last spaces remaining in the Newton Shopping Center's full parking lot, she glanced up at the lighted marquee opposite. Our Pond Is Always Frozen, it read.

The legend brought a glimmer of humor to her golden-brown eyes. Maybe this thing would be okay. She'd been doubtful when Chris had first proposed the idea. This ice rink was a forty-five minute drive from her apartment and didn't have much of a reputation.

"It's all hockey and crowded public sessions there," she'd protested.

But Chris had only shaken his blond head. "All the better. They have a clear two hours after eleven that we can rent. Don't you see the advantages? In that place we can work out routines without having spies reporting on every move we make."

Kate had merely sighed. She didn't really think any of their future competitors would be paying much attention to what they were doing, but Chris's enthusiasm was infectious.

She climbed out of her car, grabbed her overflowing leather skate bag and glanced around the dimly lit parking lot for Chris's car. But his red Corvette was nowhere in sight among the vans, station wagons and small sedans that jammed the place. Apparently she'd arrived first.

Shrugging, Kate took a tight grip on her bag, swung it over her shoulder and strode toward the entrance beneath the marquee. When she stepped inside the swinging glass doors, the lobby was deserted. Muffled noises were coming from the stairs that led down past the unattended cash register. But she didn't investigate. Instead she walked to the large Plexiglas window overlooking the rink itself and gazed out at the empty stretch of Olympic-size ice. A blue-and-white Zamboni was trundling its way along the center, scraping down the surface and then spraying water to create a smooth expanse.

As always, the sight of the newly made glassy stretch touched something inside her, and she felt a surge of adrenaline. On the drive down Kate had really wondered if she'd have the energy for a workout. After a long day in her shop, it was asking a lot to force her twenty-six-year-old body into the complex routines Chris would choreograph. But now she suddenly felt buoyed up.

Glancing around, she spotted a ladies' room and headed for it. Once she was inside, she was pleasantly surprised. Most ice-rink bathrooms were grungy holes. But this one, though not spotless and far from luxurious, was not disgusting, either. Quickly she unsnapped her padded jacket, pushed off her jeans and sweater and began to pull on a leotard and leg warmers. When she was dressed, she toted her stuffed bag outside and looked around for a place to don her skates.

There was no access onto the ice from the lobby—no changing benches, either, she noted. Obviously one had to go down the stairs past the unmanned cash register. They should have somebody up here watching the place, she thought as she made her way to the steps and started down. Anybody could just walk in.

Halfway down the staircase she clenched the railing and she stopped, frozen into immobility by the sight confronting her. Suddenly Kate realized why the parking lot had been so full. A hockey team had rented the ice that the Zamboni was cleaning, and the downstairs warming room was littered with their stuff. Hockey sticks, padded uniforms and huge gear bags lay scattered on benches and on the floor. Three of the brawny players were headed toward the stairs, dragging their equipment with them.

But that wasn't what was making Kate gape so. Directly in her line of vision was a naked man. His back was turned to her, and he was standing with his hands on his hips, holding a conversation with a partially dressed colleague. All Kate could think of was the Greek sculpture she'd admired on a visit to the Louvre years ago.

The man, a superb male specimen, seemed utterly unself-conscious in his splendid nudity. His broad, perfectly proportioned back tapered to narrow hips and firm buttocks. Dusted with darkish hair, his long muscular legs were planted wide apart. His stance was as solid as an oak's, and yet there was a vitality about him that suggested the ability to spring into action instantly.

The impressions flashing chaotically through her mind were interrupted by a hoot of raucous laughter from the trio at the foot of the stairs. The naked man's companion looked up, grinned and jabbed his friend's shoulder. Then the man himself turned his head, and Kate found herself gazing into startled, half-amused blue eyes.

Blood rushed to her cheeks and she turned and fled back up the stairs toward the sanctuary of the ladies' room. But as she put a hand on the door, she paused. Why should she be embarrassed? None of it was her fault. Glancing at her watch, she saw that it was only three minutes to eleven. She had paid for this ice time and was entitled to use the warming room. Hockey players were notorious for being boorish clods who had no consideration. Her mouth set in a stubborn line, Kate dropped her bag on the floor, sat down next to it and began to tug on her skates. At eleven on the dot she would march down there and get onto the ice no matter how many arrogant naked males stood in her path.

Ignoring the sidelong glances of two smirking hockey players who straggled past her, she doggedly tied her laces, slipped on her guards and got to her feet. She was just brushing the dirt from the floor off the back of her leotard when she sensed that someone was approaching. Turning her head, she saw a tall, well-built man in jeans and a fisherman's sweater striding across the tile floor. He had thick brown hair that was short at the sides, but it had been carelessly brushed into a wavy mop across his forehead. His nose was straight and rather narrow, as were his firm lips. With such sternly chiseled features, his lean countenance might have been harsh. But it wasn't. His mouth curled up slightly at the corners, and from the expression on his face it appeared as though he spent most of his time being amused at one thing or another.

Kate might not have recognized his features. But the eyes were another matter. She would remember those sparkling sapphire orbs anywhere. He was the naked man she'd glimpsed in the warming room.

"Maybe I don't look familiar with my clothes on," he addressed her in a pleasantly rich baritone. "But I'm the guy with the bare hindquarters."

She nodded. He was standing directly under a fluorescent light, and Kate realized from the faint lines around his eyes and mouth that he was older than she might have guessed. Thirty-one, maybe thirty-two. She was also conscious that he was eyeing her face and leotard-clad torso appreciatively. As all figure skaters do, Kate had been wearing brief workout costumes on the ice since she'd taken up the sport. Normally she was completely unself-conscious about her firmly muscled athlete's body. But suddenly she found herself vividly aware that the stretchy black fabric clinging to her high breasts and slender hips left little to the imagination.

"I wouldn't know you from the front," she heard herself say coolly, and then had to will herself not to turn red when she realized the implication.

His eyebrows began to elevate, and he put a hand to the back of his head. "Look, I'm sorry if I shocked you. But since this rink has no dressing rooms, it's part of my team's contract with the management that we get to use the warming area."

Kate raised her own fine dark eyebrows. "You and your teammates don't mind putting on a show for anyone who happens to stroll in?"

The blue eyes sparkled down at her with wicked humor. "Not if they look like you. But," he added quickly when he saw her eyes begin to narrow, "there is supposed to be someone up at the cash register to keep people out. I guess they're shorthanded tonight."

"I guess so," Kate echoed, shrugging as she picked up her bag. "Don't worry about it," she threw over her shoulder with a brief smile as she walked past him.

Admiring the curvy perfection of her body and the graceful line of her legs beneath the brightly colored leg warmers, he watched her descend the stairs and disappear around the corner. Then he scratched his head. Who was she? What was she doing here at this time of night? And how old was she? With that gamine face, she could be anywhere from eighteen to her midtwenties. But somehow he suspected she might be older than she looked. Though they'd only exchanged a few words, there'd been a maturity about her. He hoped so, anyway. He'd like to get to know her, but he was not into robbing cradles. At least not for the past few years, he thought wryly.

Just then the last of his team members, Bill O'Neill, emerged from the warming room. "I'm headed over to JK's," he called out, referring to the tavern at the other end of the shopping center where they usually winded up a practice with a couple of beers. "The other guys are already there. You coming, Sam?"

"Be with you in a couple of minutes," he told his friend. Then, still puzzling over the girl, he went down the steps and looked around. The warming room was empty. Was she out on the ice all by herself? His curiosity piqued, he shrugged on his down jacket, grabbed his gear and went back upstairs. But instead of moving toward the door and out into the night, he strode over to the Plexiglas window and looked out over the rink. What he saw compelled him to set his heavy equipment down on the floor and to put his hands on his lean hips.

She was there all right. And now he knew why she was wearing that formfitting outfit. Anyone who wanted to skate like that needed freedom of movement. Though Newton's was a hockey rink, Sam had seen plenty of figure skaters there. But outside of televised Olympic events, he couldn't remember ever seeing anyone dominate the ice like this young woman could.

Unconsciously he took a step forward and his gaze followed her fleet movements with intense concentration. Though she was slim and not very tall, she was skimming across the ice with complete confidence. Her deep back crosses in a giant figure eight pattern that covered the entire Olympic surface sent her flying with such speed that her dusky curls were whipped back from her forehead.

During that startling moment when he'd turned to find her gaping at him, her hair and unusual golden eyes had been the first thing he'd noticed. But now he was seeing a lot of other things—the lissome turn of her waist, the pertness of her tidy bottom. She was strong and apparently physically quite fearless. So many women whom he knew were strangers to their bodies. But she seemed perfectly at home in hers. Almost by habit, he found himself comparing her to another woman. They were nothing alike, but it didn't seem to matter.

He tensed slightly as he watched her next move. After one more flashing pass across the frozen expanse, she did a graceful looping turn, another back cross, and then stepped confidently into a scratch spin. It gave Sam the hollow feeling in his chest that he always got when he saw another human being doing the seemingly impossible so perfectly.

His whole concentration on the twirling dark-haired figure, Sam didn't hear the door open behind him. It came as a surprise a few minutes later when a tall blond young man joined the woman out on the ice.

Sam stiffened when he saw the intruder. Who the hell was that guy? Irrationally, he felt affronted by the man's appearance, as though the stranger had broken in on a private tête-à-tête. It wasn't long, however, before Sam had to admit that the guy was as good on skates as the girl. His warm-up covered the rink with equal speed and authority.

"Good-looking pair of kids," a jovial voice rumbled behind Sam. Don Ferguson, the rink's manager, strolled up beside him and gazed down over the ice. "How come you're still hanging around?"

Ignoring the question, Sam asked one of his own. "Who are they?"

"Kate and Chris Coleman."

Sam's head snapped around. "Married?"

"No. Brother and sister."

Relief flooded through his system, and he turned back to the window. They certainly didn't look related, and there was nothing brotherly about the way the blond guy was holding his partner. As a romantic piece of music drifted up from a tape player, he had her bent back against his arm, her supple body curved in sensual invitation. When the music ended, she flashed a beaming smile of appreciation at her handsome partner. Sam's blue eyes narrowed. Then, irritated with himself for the way he was reacting to this whole thing, he looked over at Don. "What are they doing here?"

The older man shrugged. "I had this slot free and they rented it. Said they were working on a program for a competition." He glanced down on the ice at the couple who were now waltzing to a lighthearted new piece of music. "I don't know much about figure skating, but I'd say they were ice dancers."

Sam nodded. That was it, ice dancers. Though he knew next to nothing about the sport, it had been a major event in the last Olympics. Maybe he'd have to read up on it. But just then his reverie was interrupted by a shout from the open door.

"Hey, Sam, are you coming or not? We have a beer that's going flat waiting for you."

Turning away, Sam waved at Don and flipped up the collar on his jacket against the freezing drizzle that had begun to come down outside. "Sure. I'm on my way right now."

"I'VE BEEN THINKING about this backflip all week," Chris argued. "Believe me, it's the kind of thing the judges love!"

Kate gazed up at her brother in exasperation. She loved him dearly, but when he set his sights on a target, he could be as determined and single-minded as a worker ant. He'd been like that when he was a fair-haired toddler trying to build a bigger and better castle in his sandbox, demanding that his indulgent big sister admire his efforts. And the years hadn't changed him a bit. Now that he'd decided he wanted back into the world of competitive skating, it was all he seemed to talk or think about. What's more, he seemed willing to try just about anything short of being shot out of a cannon to achieve his goal.

"But it's physically impossible, not to mention extremely dangerous for the woman," Kate protested, referring to the stunt he was now trying to talk her into. "I'm not a teenager anymore, and I'm not that flexible."

"Just relax and leave it to me. I'll do all the hard work."

She had her doubts. The move he was proposing they try was so complicated that she was still confused by it. Despite Chris's assurances, she had a strong suspicion the dazzling footwork and acrobatic twists would involve a lot of sudden spills on the ice for her before they had the move down pat. If they ever did get it right, that is.

But as always, Chris's skill and sunny confidence finally convinced her it could be done. As if her brother were a magician, the belief he inspired in her made the flip begin to happen. Although the move turned out to be possible to execute, even Chris had to admit that it certainly wasn't easy. After an hour's work Kate had fallen a number of times and was beginning to feel like an accident victim.

When Chris noticed Kate wince with pain after her latest crash landing, he was sympathetic. "Look, kid, I think we better stop before I turn you into a head-to-toe bruise," he cautioned before glancing at his watch. "Besides, we don't have much time left, anyway. I don't know about you, but I'll have a long day tomorrow."

He sighed. "There's so much work to get through at the office that I'm probably going to be squinting at a computer screen until I can't see straight."

Now it was Kate's turn to be sympathetic. Chris was such a physically active person that she'd often wondered why he'd selected computer programming as a career. Remembering what a wiggly little boy he'd been made it difficult for her to imagine him sitting still all day in front of a terminal. Perhaps it explained his determination to get back into skating.

"Actually, tomorrow is my day off," she reminded him. "The shop isn't open on Mondays. Since I'm a little shaky on some of this footwork, I think I'll stay until they throw me off the ice."

Chris shrugged and then squeezed her shoulder. "Okay, but don't overdo it." He grinned mischievously. "After all, you're not as young as you used to be."

"Don't I know it," she replied as they walked together back to the warming room. Rubbing her thigh, she pictured the fresh set of bruises that would undoubtedly appear in that tender area soon. Kate groaned. "I don't know why I let you talk me into this. I really am too old for it."

"Don't sell yourself short. I know you can do it," Chris insisted as he sat down on a bench to rapidly unlace his skates.

Kate wasn't so sure about that. But she was certain that Chris needed her help right now. His life hadn't been going too well lately. Not only did she suspect that he wasn't happy with his computer job, he'd just broken up with his girlfriend. Though Kate didn't know the details, she thought the split might have had something to do with Elise's desire to get married and her conviction that Chris was too immature to take on that sort of responsibility. Kate wasn't sure how serious he'd been about Elise or how bad he felt about losing her, and Chris wasn't telling.

Sympathetic as always to her brother's needs, she felt that moving in a new direction was important to him just now. His decision to return to competitive skating seemed to be part of that. And on such short notice, she *was* the best available partner. That, and the fact they always had fun together, was why she'd allowed him to talk her into this crazy scheme. Certainly nothing else made any sense for a person her age who was already perfectly happy with her life the way it was and who, at the moment, ached all over.

He looked up and caught her eye. "Hey, I'm excited. I really think we can do this thing."

Kate shook her head. "Maybe," she said doubtfully. "I know *you* can do it, anyway."

"Good thing I have confidence enough for both of us." He laughed and rose to his feet, swiftly removed his jersey pullover and replaced it with a clean shirt that had been folded in his bag. Once more neatly dressed, he slung a soft Italian leather jacket over his shoulder. "Well, I gotta go. Don't hang around here too long." He patted her shoulder affectionately. "And whether you believe it or not, we were great out there tonight. When we get it all together, we're going to be dynamite!"

Kate grinned and shook her head.

"Well, same time same place tomorrow night."

"Okay," she agreed, watching him stride up the stairs. As she bent over her own skates and retied them before going back out on the ice, she pictured the way his sports car would spring to life when he got behind the wheel. Chris always did things with flair and style. At this moment he was undoubtedly roaring off into the night like a rocket.

Smiling at the image, she reluctantly got up and made her way back through the metal swinging doors and out onto the deserted frozen surface. Despite Chris's confident words, she knew she was shaky on the footwork he'd choreographed. But then what normal human being wouldn't have trouble with back-cross steps designed to trip even a jet-propelled Nureyev? Yet she kept working doggedly at the complicated footwork, her concentration so total that she didn't notice the passage of time. When she finally did glance at her watch, she was surprised at the lateness of the hour. It wasn't until she got out into the warming room that she realized how sore she was. "I just hope I won't be actually crippled by tomorrow," she muttered aloud. Kate quickly removed her skates. Though she knew the manager must be around somewhere, the rink seemed as abandoned as a graveyard at midnight, and she couldn't help being a bit unnerved by the emptiness of the place. *Just call me the phantom of the ice rink*, she told herself wryly. In the ladies' room she made haste to slip out of her exercise togs and wriggle into her jeans and sweater. Casting a cursory glance at her tousled image in the mirror, she buttoned up her padded red jacket, slung her bag over her shoulder and headed for the door. But once she was outside, she paused and groaned for the second time. A freezing rain was coating all exposed surfaces with a layer of ice. Under the mercury-vapor lights the parking lot glistened a warning.

Looks like I'll have to skate home, as well, she thought grimly as she walked with great care out to her Volkswagen. Gingerly edging her way toward the car, she heard the angry whine of spinning tires as the driver of an aging Chevy attempted to back out of his iced-over parking spot. Kate grimaced. Several years ago she and Chris had been rear-ended at a traffic light in just such weather.

She had expected the lot in front of the rink to be empty, but most of the cars and trucks were still there. She wondered about that as she watched the Chevy fishtail around the corner. Hadn't the hockey people gone home yet? The speculation made her think of the blue-eyed man in the warming room. She shook her head. The guy had really been something else! But although he was a hockey player and she tended to classify that group as a pack of violent macho dolts, he didn't seem to fit the mold. There had been too much intelligent humor sparkling deep in those remarkable blue eyes.

A disconcerting image of him as he'd looked in the warming room presented itself to her mind as she reached out to insert her key in the door lock. But then all such wayward thoughts vanished. The door was coated with ice, and the lock appeared to be frozen.

"Oh, my God," Kate muttered. She went around to the passenger side and tried that door with the same result. "Damn," she exclaimed, looking around a little wildly at the dark and glistening parking lot. The freezing rain showed no sign of letting up. Suddenly the lighted marquee over the ice rink blinked out, which meant, she supposed, that the place was shutting down for the night.

"Damn!" she repeated, and this time the exclamation had a slightly desperate edge. Determinedly Kate bent over the lock and struggled to jam her key into it. But her efforts were in vain. The thing wouldn't budge. Silently she cursed her luck and then glanced down the row of storefronts lining the shopping center. From what she could see, only one appeared to be open—a tavern named JK's. Frowning, Kate shouldered her bag and trudged toward it. Maybe someone could give her some help. At the very least, there would be a phone there.

But when she walked inside the place, her courage failed her slightly. Filled with cigarette smoke, reeking of beer, the bar was noisy with the rumbling sounds of men's voices. A roar of male amusement punctuated the background din, and to her dismay Kate caught sight of a round table in the center of the room. It was occupied by the hockey players she'd encountered earlier. Directly in her line of vision was the blue-eyed man, his head thrown back in laughter. He'd spot her any minute. Averting her face, she headed for the bar.

"Can I help you, miss?"

"Do you have a de-icer, by any chance?"

The man in the white apron standing behind the taps looked puzzled. "De-icer?"

Kate shifted her bag, which was beginning to feel like the weight of the world on her shoulders. "I'm having a problem with with my car. The lock is frozen."

Slowly the bartender shook his head. "No. Sorry I can't help you. Though one of our customers might have one," he added. "Do you want to ask around?"

That was the last thing Kate wanted to do. "Well, look, maybe you could give me some matches That might help." A ludicrous vision of herself playing poor little match girl flew through her mind. But maybe holding a flame to the frozen lock was worth a try.

Looking doubtful, the bartender reached into a box under the counter and came up with several matchbooks. As Kate held a hand out for them, she felt a tap on her shoulder.

"Sounds like you're having trouble. Can I help?"

Kate jerked around to find herself once more looking into blue eyes. Only this time they were disconcertingly close.

"I'm Sam Ryder, by the way." The man who had touched more than her thoughts this evening held out a hand, and she found her cold fingers being swallowed in a warm, dry palm.

For a fleeting instant she sensed that he expected her to recognize his name. But it didn't ring a bell. "Kate Coleman," she responded.

"I heard you say you couldn't get your car open. Why don't I come out and see what I can do?"

Before she had time to gather her wits and murmur a protest, he had turned away. Grabbing a jacket from the back of his chair, he left an offhand explanation with his friends. She hardly had time to bridle at the knowing expression on one or two beer-flushed faces before he lifted the heavy skate bag from her shoulders, clipped a hard hand around her elbow and ushered her firmly out the door.

"Rotten night," he commented as he guided her back toward her car.

That was an understatement. The roads, she suspected, were going to be solid ice all the way home.

"Do you have snow tires?" he inquired.

She shook her head, concentrating on her feet as she slipped and slid across the parking lot. Once they were in front of the rink, she pointed at her dark green Volkswagen, which appeared to be huddling like an unhappy turtle under its dense coat of ice. "I hadn't gotten around to putting the snow tires on," she told him. "I wasn't expecting weather like this for another month or so."

He nodded. His shoulders were hunched under his upturned collar, and as he bent to examine the car door, beads of water in his dark curls caught the rays of an overhead mercury-vapor light and sparkled. "The lock's frozen, all right. But this might do the trick," he said, producing a substantial-looking steel lighter and striking the flint.

"I haven't seen one like that in years!" Kate exclaimed. "It's a vintage Zippo, isn't it?"

He shot her a surprised look. "Yes, it was my grandfather's. How did you know?"

She shrugged. "I'm interested in things like that."

Still holding the flame close to the lock, he withdrew a pipe cleaner from the pocket of his jacket and threaded it into the frozen aperture. After probing several times, he took it out and turned to Kate.

"Give me your key."

Obediently she did as he requested, and in the next moment he was opening the door easily and stowing her skate bag in the back seat. Then he slid in under the steering wheel, adjusted the seat as far back as it would go, and reached across to unlock the passenger door.

"Come on in and get out of the rain."

"But . . ."

"Come on!"

Frowning slightly, she opened the passenger door and sat down. Sam Ryder was a big man, and inside the cramped interior she felt rather overwhelmed by the fact. "Look, thanks for your help. I appreciate it, but..."

"Better make sure your car starts," he murmured, turning the key in the ignition. The engine sprang to life with a satisfying growl. "Sounds healthy," he commented, switching on the headlights.

"I had it tuned last week." She glanced at his shadowy profile, and a little tremor shivered down her spine. "Hadn't you better get back to your friends now? I'm grateful, but I can take it from here."

He shook his head. "It's going to be dangerous on the roads tonight. I won't feel right until I've seen you safely home. Tell me where you live."

"But what about your car?"

He twisted the upper part of his body and craned his head to back out. As he made the manuever, his right arm rested on the top of her seat, and she felt the damp cloth of his parka brush against her neck.

"I didn't bring my car," he informed her. "I rode with a friend."

"But . . . but," she sputtered, "how are you going to get home?"

"Don't worry about it. I'll take a cab."

"At this time of night? And in this weather? Look, really, I'm perfectly capable of driving myself. This isn't necessary!"

"I think it is. Now, where do you live?" He was looking at her with the patient but implacable air of a man who intends to get his way. Suddenly Kate realized that she was more than a little frightened by the icy roads. But were they more dangerous than this man?

She eyed him, trying to assess the situation. Even though he played hockey, Sam Ryder didn't look like the violent type, and all the people in the bar had seen her leave with him. So chances were that she was safe enough.

On the other hand, she didn't feel particularly secure. There was an "atmosphere" between herself and this man. It had been there from that first galvanizing moment when she'd seen him standing so magnificently naked. But now in the confined dark interior of her car with the rain beating outside, it was a tangible thing. Though they probably had nothing in common, he was physically very appealing. She was attracted and, she suspected, so was he.

A disturbing blend of excitement laced with wary apprehension fluttered inside her. If she let him drive her home, what would happen when they got to her place? But suddenly she decided to throw caution to the wind. She'd wait until they arrived to find out.

"I live in Ellicott City," she told him. "On Main Street."

If she had expected him to be put off by the distance, she was disappointed. "Okay" was all he said as he headed her beloved bug cautiously out onto the icy road.

2

"WHERE DO YOU LIVE?" Kate finally asked. They had been riding in silence for several minutes while Sam concentrated on his driving. But now he'd pulled onto a main road where conditions appeared somewhat better.

"In Baltimore, near the harbor."

Kate stared at his strong profile. That was at least half an hour going the other way from the rink. Between driving her home and getting back to his own place, the man was going to be up half the night.

"Look, really," she began to protest all over again. "I feel bad about putting you to so much trouble."

"Don't. I'm enjoying myself," he returned. He shot her a grin, and she caught a brief glimpse of white teeth and glinting eyes in the darkness. "I tend to say what I'm thinking, so I'll admit that I want to get to know you. This gives me a perfect opportunity."

Kate squirmed slightly. "Well, that's being honest."

"Why not? You knew it anyway, didn't you?"

She was a bit disconcerted to find herself being equally honest. "Yes."

Kate's cheeks suddenly felt hot, and she didn't look at him. But when the car came to a slow sliding stop in front of a traffic light, she knew he was studying her.

"Well, since we're stuck with each other, at least until I get you home," he murmured, "how about telling me something about yourself?"

"Like what?"

"Like how did you learn to skate like Dorothy Hamill?"

While she digested the interesting fact that he'd been watching her on the ice, the light turned green, and he changed gear and accelerated cautiously.

"My brother and I were raised by an aunt who was a figure-skating fan. She put me on the ice when I was seven years old, and I've been skating ever since."

"And how long is that?"

She gave him a sidelong glance, and he grinned. "Nosy bastard, aren't I?"

"I'm twenty-six."

Smoothly he pulled onto the beltway where the slick freezing rain had been ground to harmless slush by fast-moving traffic. "You don't look more than twenty."

Kate made a face in the dark. People were always saying that. "Right now I feel about ninety."

He slanted her a sharp look. "I noticed you were limping when we walked out to the car. Did you hurt yourself?"

"I'm out of training. I took several falls during practice, and they're beginning to catch up with me." She shifted in her seat, trying for a more comfortable position.

"What kind of a skater are you, anyway? Are you a professional?"

She shook her head. "No. When I finished with amateur competition, I went to college and got interested in other things. I never did turn pro."

"How about the guy you were with? He's your brother, isn't he?"

Kate nodded. "He didn't turn pro, either, though he's thinking about it." She cocked her head. Maybe it was time to counter Sam Ryder's curiosity with one or two questions of her own.

"I have the feeling I'm being grilled. Are you a detective or an investigative reporter, or what?"

Laughing, he angled the VW toward the exit ramp. "Sorry. Am I being that obnoxious? I'm a sportswriter. I write for the *Baltimore Globe*."

Kate turned toward him. Now she knew why he might have thought she'd recognize his name. "I've never seen your byline because I don't take the *Globe*. I subscribe to the *Washington Post*."

"Snob."

It was said in a teasing tone, so Kate merely laughed. "Could be."

Chris called her a snob from time to time, actually. And maybe it was true. Her tastes had never been conventional. Unlike so many of her peers, she didn't care for discos or daring clothes and wouldn't be caught dead in a singles' bar. Her idea of good music was the chamber variety, and fun for her was a concert, a play or a good novel. As a teenager she'd been too busy working out on the ice to chase boys. And in college she'd been more interested in her fine-arts courses than in looking around for someone to marry.

She'd always been selective about men. Perhaps she was too much of a romantic—wanting it her way or not at all. However, that didn't mean she wasn't going to be attracted to a good-looking male who dropped out of the sky in front of her. And she was very conscious that something like that had happened tonight. The man so capably driving her VW was arousing feelings inside her that were both exciting and more than a little disturbing.

But true to her conservative nature, she had no intention of letting him in on that. "How long have you lived in Baltimore?" she questioned.

"Maybe six years. How about you?" He glanced at her face, which was only a dim oval in the car's intimate darkness. "How long have you lived here?"

"In Ellicott City, only three years. But in the Baltimore area, all my life. My parents' house was on Greenspring Avenue."

"Was?"

"They were killed in a car accident when Chris and I were little, and the property was sold."

"I'm sorry. That must have been tough. Is that when you moved in with your aunt?"

"Yes." Kate laced her fingers together in her lap, and they were both silent for several minutes.

"Where exactly do you live?" Sam asked as the car coasted down the steep hill that sheltered the valley where the historic little enclave nestled. Once a flourishing mill town and the site of the oldest B & O Railway terminus in America, Ellicott City was now a quaint sightseers' paradise. The old stone buildings on the steeply pitched main street housed restaurants, craft stores and antique shops. One of these latter belonged to Kate.

"You'll have to park on the street," she explained as the automobile cruised slowly up the narrow lane. Midway up the hill she pointed to the sign above her shop. "I live there."

Sam Ryder shot her a curious glance. "You live at Blithe Spirits?"

Kate refused to apologize for the fanciful name she'd picked for her store. "The shop is mine. I live above it."

"Interesting," he murmured, extricating his long legs and climbing out. As he came around to Kate's side of the car, he stole a quick glance into the darkened storefront. The display window held dishes, glassware and a few carefully selected brass and silver items. It was too dark to see into the interior of the place. "How long have you been the proprietor?" he asked as he helped her out.

"Three years." She winced as she spoke. It was a bit of a struggle to wriggle out of the low seat. Her leg had stiffened up and her hip was definitely feeling sore. "I guess you'd better come in with me to call your cab."

He nodded and followed her around to the side of the building where she began to climb a set of steep wooden steps. Ice had formed on them and they were slippery.

"Three years? Was it rough getting started?"

"It wasn't easy." Actually, she mused, the store was doing pretty well now. When she'd first opened it, all her friends had been skeptical. But she'd surprised them all. Her fanciful blend of brass and glass appealed to the tourists who visited Ellicott City on the weekends, and during the past three years she'd carved out what she considered to be a very satisfactory life for herself.

"You're limping," Sam commented behind her. "You're walking more like a beat-up hockey player than a beautiful young figure skater. Are you sure you're all right?"

"Oh, I'm fine." She shook her head and her tousled curls caught a stray finger of moonlight that had managed to filter through the thick cloud cover. "Skaters fall all the time. It's part of the business."

"Well, I know hockey players do. But we wear armor. You were out there with practically nothing on."

As she fished in her purse for her key, she shot him a look. "Just how much time did you spend watching me, anyway?"

"Enough to know that I liked what I saw," he informed her with no sign of embarrassment.

Slightly flustered by this remark, Kate pushed open the door, flipped on the light and motioned him inside. Gesturing to the right, she pointed to a 1930 vintage wall telephone, complete with brass bells and a varnished oak case. "That phone works. Why don't you call your cab?"

Sam's eyebrows shot up, and he walked slowly toward the ancient apparatus. Do I say 'Hello Central'?"

Amused, Kate shook her head. "No, just try dialing the number."

"I'm not sure I remember how. I'm at my best with push buttons." As he spoke, he flipped through the phone book. Then his swift fingers dialed the number.

He stood with his broad back to her, and she admired his elegant build. Once again she was disturbed when the image of how he'd looked naked flashed through her mind. Blinking, she forcibly banished it. Such thoughts were too intimate for their present circumstances. It was late at night, and they were alone together in her apartment.

After a moment he hung up and turned to face her. "There's a lot of icy roads everywhere. The state highway patrol closed the road to Columbia. But the Baltimore Pike is still open, and the cab should be here in half an hour."

Kate glanced over his dark head at the school clock on the wall. It was now close to 2:00 A.M. Attractive as this stranger was, she was feeling more and more odd about the situation. He had taken her home safely, however, and she couldn't very well tell him to leave. Clearing her throat, she said, "Can I offer you a cup of coffee?"

He hesitated for a few seconds and then started to unsnap his jacket. Absurdly, the simple movements made her feel like looking away. "Yes, thank you," he was saying. "I don't like keeping you up, but I can't leave till the cab comes."

"No problem. Excuse me a minute." Quickly removing her own jacket and hanging it on the antique coatrack by the door, she went into the kitchen.

Left alone in the living room, Sam looked around curiously. What he saw was not what he'd come to expect from his experience with women Kate's age. Instead of black leather and square-edged chrome furniture, he found himself surrounded by a whimsical and eclectic mix of valuable antiques and humorous junk. The Chippendale-style couch by the living-room window was genuine, he suspected. And the collection of French snuff boxes arranged on a shelf above it suggested care and knowledge on the part of its owner. Sam knew the Burma Shave signs on the opposite wall were real because he recognized them from his childhood.

Smiling, he turned away. Then his eye was caught by a lawyer's bookcase that had been directly behind him.

Crossing the room, he knelt to study the volumes it held.

When Kate came back to announce that the coffee was ready, she found him seated on the floor, examining her copy of *The Raven* with the Doré engravings.

"This is nicely bound," he observed, glancing up at her with a slow smile that had an odd effect on her solar plexus.

"Yes," she volunteered and was surprised and pleased that her voice sounded steady. "I picked it up at an auction, but it's not worth as much as I thought."

He nodded. "Yes, I know. If you look at the background of the pictures, you can see that these etchings are copies of the Doré originals. They're not done from his plates, but from wooden copies."

Kate was amazed. "How do you happen to know so much about Doré engravings?" That sort of expertise was the last thing she might have expected from a hockey jock.

Carefully replacing the volume, he stood up in a single graceful movement and grinned down at her, his blue eyes twinkling. "I like old books. As a matter of fact, I collect them, especially humor—everything from Lewis Carroll and Artemus Ward to Woody Allen and Steve Martin."

Kate laughed. "Goodness, that sounds like quite a broad interest."

As they entered the kitchen, he paused to inhale deeply. The air was fragrant with the aroma of fresh-brewed coffee. "Smells great," he commented. "What brand do you use?"

"It's a special mix called Blue Jamaican that they sell down the street." Surreptitiously Kate rubbed the sore place on her hip.

Sam was gazing at her with open speculation. "I bet your closet doesn't have a single pink polyester pant suit in it."

"What do you mean?" Kate was startled.

"I mean that, so far as I can tell, everything about you has been very carefully picked for quality."

"You make me sound like a fussy old maid."

He regarded her consideringly, and the corners of his mouth twitched. "Certainly not old. Fussy perhaps." Sam leaned against the counter and inspected his surroundings, taking in the polished copper and carefully refinished ash table with turned legs. "But mostly just very, very careful," he finished with a roguish lilt in his deep voice.

Kate flushed slightly as she accepted the truth of his observation. She was not extravagant, but she'd always been partial to having things just the way she wanted them—and not just material objects, but the whole manner in which she conducted her life. "I know what I like," she said a bit defensively. "And when I can afford it, I get it."

Sam only grinned. "Why not?" Pulling out a chair, he sat down and stretched out his legs. Watching him warily, she poured them each a mug of coffee.

"Cream or sugar?"

When he shook his head, she slid a mug across the table to him. As she completed the simple operation, she found herself staring into his eyes. An intense shade of royal blue, they were disconcertingly alert beneath the screen of his thick dark lashes. She couldn't remember meeting anyone else with eyes so strikingly beautiful. There was, Kate noted, a dark stubble on his chin where his beard was beginning to reassert itself. But it didn't make him any less attractive—quite the contrary. His evident virility only heightened his appeal.

Despite herself, her gaze dropped lower, and she noted that his jeans, which stretched tightly across his flat belly, were so worn that they were threadbare at the knees. But the thick fisherman's sweater that covered his wide shoulders was no bargain-basement special. He lifted his cup to his lips, and she caught the rich glint of gold on his arm. Around his sinewy, slightly hairy right wrist he was wearing a handsomely crafted chain.

"I like that gold chain," she dropped the words into the silence between them. "It looks like *it's* been very carefully selected."

To her surprise he reddened slightly, and for a moment he looked uncomfortable. Sam was thinking of the woman who'd given it to him. He didn't want to be reminded of her just now.

"Thanks. I'm curious about your skating," he said, abruptly changing the subject. "Whatever you and your brother were doing out there on the ice looked very impressive, but what exactly was it?"

Kate wondered what there was about the gold chain that made him sensitive. But she didn't pursue the subject. Taking another sip from her mug, she hid a dry smile. How typical, she was thinking. This man was a sportswriter, yet he didn't know the first thing about figure skating—a sport whose world and Olympic champions had frequently been his own countrymen.

"It's ice dancing," she explained. "Chris and I are planning to compete in the regionals next month. We're working on our original set pattern and free dance."

He shook his head. "Somehow I had the impression that it was only teenage kids who did that sort of thing."

"That's true in freestyle. I gave up amateur competition when I was eighteen, and Chris was twenty when he quit. But dance is different." Kate looked down into her coffee. She noticed with annoyance that her hand shook slightly and she hastily set the cup down. Was she jittery because she was tired, or did it have something to do with the man lounging at her table? She suspected it was the latter and wished his cab would come. Perhaps it was the late hour or the icy night beyond the black windows, but isolated with each other in the tiny, intimate world of her kitchen, they seemed totally cut off from the outside. And the fact was beginning to get to her.

"You seem nervous," Sam said, suddenly startling her. "Is something wrong?"

"No. I'm just tired."

Her denial had been too quick.

"Maybe you feel a little awkward about entertaining a strange man in your apartment this late at night," he suggested with an understanding smile. "Well, you have nothing to worry about."

"Why?" Kate gave him a sharp look. "Are you harmless?"

His smile widened, and he shook his head. "I wouldn't say that. But fear not. Though I'm not harmless, I am safe."

Not feeling safe at all, Kate looked down at her hands again. "In dance," she said, continuing their earlier conversation, "competitors are older. It's a branch of the sport that takes greater maturity."

"What's the difference?" He seemed genuinely interested, and despite her innate reserve, Kate found herself preaching her favorite sermon.

"Dance is more like ballet, whereas freestyle is more like gymnastics. There are no throws or jumps in dance. But the footwork is much tighter and much more dangerous."

Sam settled back in his chair as though he planned to stay there for a while. "You said you were a competitor when you were younger. Did you win any titles?"

"I was a National Junior Ladies Champion, and as a Senior Lady I was an alternate for the Olympics—but I never got to go."

He whistled. "Very impressive."

Kate met his clear gaze and smiled briefly. She supposed it was impressive. But when she'd quit, she'd been ready to give up the long hours of practice and the brief moments of glory in order to go on to something else. That hadn't been the case with Chris. Because he'd never mastered consistent triple jumps, he'd lost important competitions. When he'd stopped competing, he'd retired from skating but never really moved on to anything else he found equally satisfying.

"The medals I won as a kid don't make me ache any less now," Kate said ruefully.

"Well, you looked good out there to me." Sam offered her a small salute with his empty mug. "I wish you luck."

"Thank you." Kate shifted restlessly in her chair and glanced at her watch. "You're the one who's going to need luck with that cab. It's almost three o'clock."

He looked surprised, as though he hadn't noticed the time passing. "I'll give the company another call."

At that moment the sound of squealing tires and a racing motor was followed by a loud crash. Ignoring the pain in her leg, Kate ran to the living room and peered out the window. Looking down at Main Street two stories below, she saw by the light of the streetlamps that a white pickup had skidded down the hill and ultimately came to rest sideways in the middle of the street. A second later a disgruntled looking young man in a plaid lumber jacket got out and walked around his vehicle, slipping and sliding on what was obviously a layer of ice.

Sam had joined Kate at the window. He was standing directly behind her, and she could feel the warmth of his large body only a few inches from hers.

"It looks worse out there," he commented.

"Yes," she agreed, her eyes following the progress of the pickup. Its driver had started it up again and was inching very carefully toward a parking space.

"I would go out and help the guy," Sam was saying, and she was very aware of his warm breath against the top of her head. "But it looks like he can take care of himself."

"I recognize him, actually. It's Phil Maclett. He owns the craft shop across the street and lives above it."

"You all must be quite a chummy group here." Sam's voice was surprisingly gruff, and Kate swiveled around to give him a questioning look. But when they were face-to-face, he was so close, his tall, lean body within inches of hers, that she felt an unnerving tremor ripple up her spine. Her coppery gaze was drawn into his, and she saw that his pupils were dilated. She supposed hers must be, too. It was shadowy next to the window.

Feeling the need to escape, she moved away. "Not really," she started to say. But just then she felt a sharp stab of pain in her leg and almost toppled over on the floor.

Sam was very quick. He caught her when she was only halfway down. "What's wrong?"

"I don't know. My leg . . ."

"Here." Lifting her bodily, he crossed the room in three swift strides. The next thing she knew, he was settling her gently on the couch.

"It's nothing, really," Kate began to protest. "My muscles are sore, and my leg just stiffened up on me."

"Where does it hurt?" Sam was half crouching, half kneeling on the floor in front of her.

"Right here." She pointed to a place below her knee.

He touched a finger to the spot she'd indicated and then began to roll up her pant leg.

Kate put a hand out as though to stop him. "Really, that's not—" But it was too late. His warm palm was already cradling the smooth swell of her calf.

"I can feel a knot there." He began to rub it with slow, soothing strokes.

Kate struggled with confusion. He evidently knew what he was doing because his touch was very pleasant. But at the same time she was disturbed by the situation.

Sam seemed to read her mind. "Relax," he told her in a gentle voice. "I told you, I'm safe. I'm not going to hurt you." His fingers circled knowingly on the fleshy swell. "Doesn't that feel good?"

"Yes, it does," she had to admit.

"All right, then. Lean back and enjoy."

Kate found herself doing as he requested. She relaxed against the back of the couch and closed her eyes. In a moment the only sound in the room was the patter of freezing rain against the windowpane and the rhythmic ticking of the clock. As Sam's hands continued to work on her, warm tingles of pleasure mixed very slightly with pain were the only sensations of which she was aware. Unconsciously she parted her lips slightly and sighed.

Sam smiled up at Kate, enjoying the new angle from which he was seeing her and thinking how pretty she looked. Her lips were pink and soft, and a dark curl had slipped over her forehead in a very fetching manner. "See, doesn't that feel better?" he murmured.

"Yes."

"What you really need is a good allover massage."

Kate's eyes flew open, and she found that he had slid up onto the cushion next to her. Before she had time to react to that, his hands were on her shoulders.

"You're as tense as a newly strung tennis racket," he informed her. "Why? Is something bothering you?"

"Right now it is."

His blue eyes danced. "What?"

Kate was finding it difficult to breathe, but she met his unnerving sapphire gaze squarely. "You."

He smiled, and she noticed inanely that he had perfect teeth. Orthodontia as a kid, she decided.

He moved closer so that their faces were within inches. "Are you worried that I might try to kiss you?"

"Very worried." Her voice sounded so breathless that it was unrecognizable. She was suddenly very aware of his after-shave. It was a resinous, mossy fragrance that seemed to fill her head like an early-morning breeze from a pine forest.

"Kate," he was saying, "you're an athlete. You know the best way to conquer an irrational fear is to go ahead and try the thing that's got you buffaloed. That way you find out there's nothing to be afraid of."

"Or there's lots to be afraid of," she countered just before his lips closed over hers.

At first she did nothing—just tasted the feel of his firm mouth on hers. It was very pleasant, and then as he moved from one corner of her lips to the other, coaxing and tasting, she found herself beginning to respond. As he pulled her close, her hands went up to his shoulders. Through the rich thickness of his sweater, she could feel the solid structure of his back and arms. There was a wiry strength in them that she could sense even though he wasn't exerting it.

His mouth moved from her lips to her jaw and then up to her ear. "See, that wasn't so bad," he whispered.

"No, but I have the feeling you're just getting started," she managed.

Sam chuckled. "Keep in mind that I never claimed to be harmless. I don't like to begin something without finishing it. Kissing you wouldn't be complete without running my hands through some of those curls." He reached up and twined a finger in her hair. "Mmm, it's as soft as it looks."

Kate opened her eyes and found herself staring directly into the melting indigo depths of his. "How does it look?"

His response was immediate. "Like black silk."

She'd been wanting to run her fingers through his hair and now she did. Moving one hand from his shoulders to the back of his neck, she touched the thick, vital strands. Sensing the hesitant movement of her fingers, he smiled again. Then his lips returned to hers. She had expected the kiss to be more insistent, demanding some sort of surrender. But it wasn't and it didn't. Instead, his mouth continued to persuade, teasing and tantalizing her until she found herself smiling with the pleasure of his gentle touch—and wanting more.

When Sam finally lifted his head from hers, Kate's cheeks were flushed, and her eyes were bright with laughter and excitement.

"You're fun to kiss, Ms Coleman," he informed her solemnly.

"You're pretty good at it yourself. You've obviously done a fair amount."

"True," he agreed with a suddenly wry expression. "But I've never before had the pleasure of rubbing noses with a figure skater."

She laughed at that. "Is that your idea of what we were doing?"

"I suspect that a nice girl like you doesn't want to hear all my ideas about what we were doing."

The sparkle in Sam's expressive eyes was all at once so wicked that Kate found her gaze dropping to his firm chin with its dusting of sandpapery stubble. "Maybe you'd better check on that cab," she murmured.

"Maybe I'd better," he agreed, sounding amused.

Releasing her, he got off the couch and strode across the room to the phone. He'd taken his warmth with him, and Kate found herself regretting her prudence. She'd have liked one more kiss from Sam Ryder, she thought a bit giddily.

But when he turned away from the telephone, his expression sobered her.

"I'm afraid you're stuck with me for a while longer, Kate. There won't be any cab tonight. The state police have closed the roads indefinitely."

3

KATE'S JAW SAGGED. "You mean you can't get out of here?"

"'Fraid not." Sam jammed his hands in the pockets of his jeans and tilted his head to study his reluctant hostess's expression. "You don't look overjoyed."

She immediately closed her mouth and raised her hands palm up. "I'm sorry. It's just—"

"Just that you're not in the habit of entertaining strange men all night. You don't have to tell me that. It's been obvious from the first."

"What's that supposed to mean?"

His grin was mischievous. "Only that you've got 'nice girl' written all over you." He put up a hand. "Don't look insulted. I happen to like nice girls. Even better, I'm a nice guy, so we're well matched."

"Well matched for what?"

"For spending the night together."

His expression was so cheeky that Kate started to laugh. "Well, maybe I didn't look overjoyed, but you don't exactly look miserable, either."

"The only misery-producing feature of this situation for me is that I'll be sleeping out here on the floor while you'll be in your bedroom with the door locked, barred and a chair tilted against the knob."

His casual joke not only put most of her qualms to rest, but made her smile. "I've got a rollaway cot and a sleeping bag, so you won't be all that uncomfortable."

"Perfect." Sam came forward and took her hand. "How are you feeling? Are you okay now?"

Kate blinked in confusion and then realized that he was referring to her leg. "Oh, yes, I'm fine. I'll just be a little stiff tomorrow, that's all." She eased herself off the couch and walked across the room toward the hall and the linen closet. "As a matter of fact," she added, looking back over her shoulder, "I have a pair of men's pajamas and a bathrobe you can use. Would you like me to get them for you?"

The pleasant smile on Sam's face was suddenly wiped clean. "What?"

Realizing what must be going through his mind, Kate issued a quick denial. "Oh, it's not from a former lover or anything. My brother sometimes spends the night here."

Sam's good humor was instantly restored. "That sounds fine."

Fifteen minutes later she left her unexpected guest setting up the cot and unrolling the sleeping bag.

Once she was in her bedroom, Kate shut the paneled oak door firmly behind her. For a moment she stood eyeing the lock. It was old-fashioned, but it still worked. Then feeling slightly ridiculous, she shook her head. Did she really think that Sam Ryder was going to come bursting in on her in the middle of the night?

The answer was no. Nevertheless, she ended up by tipping a straight chair against the knob. Kate's Aunt Pam had been a very careful woman who cautioned her pretty niece daily against the dangers besetting the young girls of this world. You never escape your child-hood, Kate thought dryly as she remembered all the warnings her favorite relative had drummed into her.

She was embarrassed by her precautions when Sam tapped on her bedroom door a few minutes later. "What is it?" she called out. "Do you need anything?"

"I just wanted to say good-night."

"Good night, Sam."

She could hear the smile in his voice. "Just out of curiosity, do you wear long flannel nightgowns?"

Kate looked down at the prim rosebud-dotted gown that swept her feet.

"You're not saying anything, so that means you do. I bet you have the door barricaded, too."

"No," Kate lied.

"Hmm. I don't know whether to be flattered or insulted."

"What do you mean by that?"

He chuckled. "Never mind. Sleep tight, Kate."

She heard the faint creak of the wood floor as he retreated down the hall. After that the apartment was silent.

Tucked in her bed, Kate lay wide-eyed, looking out the window and listening to the whispery ping of sleet against the panes. Though she was exhausted, she knew it would be a while before she'd get to sleep. Too much adrenaline was pumping through her system.

This had certainly been an unusual day, she decided. There was the excitement of starting this new regime of practice with Chris. She'd been pampering herself with a safe, comfortable existence. Working every night on a competitive dance routine was going to change things. But there was more to the breathless feeling in her chest than that. A lot of it, she knew, related directly to the attractive man resting in her living room.

As the night deepened and the freezing rain continued to coat the world outside, Kate's thoughts darted about like snowballs in a children's free-for-all. One moment she thought about the strangeness of her meeting with Sam Ryder, and the next she mentally ran through complicated dance routines. But when she finally did drop off to sleep, it was a pair of twinkling blue eyes that invaded her dreams, not ice-dance patterns.

Though Kate hadn't bothered to set her alarm, it was her habit to awaken early. When her eyelids opened in the gray light of an overcast morning, she closed them firmly again. But she couldn't remain comfortably snuggled under the blankets for long. There was too much going on inside her head. What was Sam Ryder doing, she wondered. Though she listened carefully, she couldn't hear a sound inside the apartment. Finally unable to contain her curiosity, she swung her feet down to the chilly floor, stepped into bedroom slippers and pulled on a fleecy pink bathrobe.

Her muscles had stiffened up badly during the night, and she groaned as she hobbled to the window and peered out. Though there was still ice on the sidewalks, it had already melted on the street.

Turning, she made her way to the door, smiled ruefully at her own foolishness as she dislodged the chair and then turned the knob and poked her head out. The hall was empty. Speedily she crossed it and disappeared into the bathroom opposite her room. A few minutes later she reemerged, looked quickly to her right and left and then vanished once more into the sanctuary of her bedroom, where she spent the next twenty minutes doing some mild limbering-up exercises. Another ten were devoted to putting on makeup and brushing her hair with more than her usual attention. When she was finally dressed in jeans and a fluffy mauve sweater, she ventured out again.

Uncertainly Kate glanced to her right. The kitchen was at the other end of the hall, so there was really no reason to go into the living room. But she hadn't heard a sound from her guest in hours, and curiosity was getting the better of her. Had he gotten up in the middle of the night and left? She supposed that was possible. If road conditions had improved, he could have simply called a cab and departed.

Cautiously she tiptoed toward the archway. Because it was on the side of the building that didn't catch the morning sun, the living room was darker than her bedroom. Her anxious expression softened into a smile as she studied the picture Sam made. He was half in and half out of the sleeping bag, and some of his tousled brown locks had fallen forward over his brow. It wasn't difficult to imagine how he'd looked as a youngster. Damned attractive, she thought wryly. Except that now the beginnings of a beard shadowed the rather aggressive line of his jaw. He hadn't bothered to put on her brother's pajamas, which lay neatly folded on a nearby chair. His shoulders were bare and, very possibly, so was the rest of him.

Her admiring gaze lingered on him. But when he stirred, she hastily drew back. It wouldn't do to have the man open those laughing blue eyes of his and find her gaping at him.

Kate walked quietly back down the hall to the kitchen. It was surprisingly bright at the eastern end of the apartment, and when she went to the sink and squinted out the window, she saw that rays of sunlight were beginning to pierce the overcast sky. If the cloud cover was dissipating, what remained of the ice would probably be gone in an hour or so, she conjectured.

After she'd filled the coffee maker with water and freshly ground beans, she switched on the small television set she kept in the kitchen. Kate didn't usually watch TV at night, but she did enjoy tuning in to the news while she ate her breakfast in the morning.

She was just in time to hear a local weather report that confirmed her own observations. "The effects of last night's unseasonably early freeze were all but gone by 7:00 A.M. this morning. Major and secondary roads are now safe for travel" the forecaster was saying.

When he'd finished his summary, Kate got up to make toast and scrambled eggs. The aroma of brewing coffee was already whetting her appetite. She liked substantial breakfasts and suspected that Sam Ryder might, too. As she puttered around the stove, she left the television set on. There was a popular national news program that she enjoyed catching if she could.

The program's attractive co-anchor was Carol Langford. She'd left Baltimore a few months back to take a position with the network's morning show. Since then Kate, a longtime admirer of the blond newswoman, had followed her career with interest. It was always gratifying to see a female of whom one could really feel proud—and never mind the fact she was from Kate's hometown. Kate considered her to be capable and intelligent, as well as beautiful and charming. She

deserved her success, and Kate was getting a small vi-
carious thrill watching her achieve it.

The camera had just homed in on Carol's elegantly
patrician features when Kate heard the creak of footsteps in the hall. A moment later Sam wandered into
the kitchen.

Kate hid a smile. The man was apparently not the
clear-eyed type in the morning. Though he'd tied her
brother's bathrobe around his lean hips, he had a rum-
pled, disoriented look that was almost comical. A
wayward lock of hair hung down over his forehead,
and his eyes were heavy from sleep.

Running a hand over his sandpapery jaw and then
through his tousled hair, he mumbled, "Is that fresh
coffee I smell?"

"It certainly is," Kate returned cheerfully. Morning
had always been her best time. That was one of the
reasons why working out late at night with Chris was
going to be a drag.

For a moment Sam looked bemused and even half-
insulted by her chipper demeanor. But then, chuckling
at himself, he started to issue a grateful reply. Just then,
however, he was distracted as the sound of Carol
Langford's pleasant contralto penetrated his early-
morning fog. His head swiveled sharply, and he stared
at the set. As he focused on the blonde's attractive image on the screen, his body stiffened and his blue eyes
narrowed. All at once there was a cold set to his face.

"May I turn it off?" he asked. The question was rhe-
torical. He was already striding to the small television,
and when he reached it he flicked the switch with an
abrupt movement. "I can't take bright-eyed news faces
in the morning." Then he added tightly, "I'd like to

shower and shave. Will I find a razor in the bath-room?''

Kate, who'd been watching with surprise from her position in front of the stove, nodded. ''On the bottom shelf in the medicine cabinet.''

As he walked quickly from the room, she stared after him, still startled by the change in his expression. One moment he'd been a pleasantly sleepy-eyed guest and the next a grim-faced stranger. Apparently Mr. Ryder was a more mercurial character than she'd realized. Troubled by his inexplicable behavior, she turned back to the frying pan on the stove and began scooping creamy scrambled eggs from it onto a plate.

When Sam emerged from the bathroom fifteen min-utes later freshly showered, shaved and dressed in his jeans and sweater, his Jekyll-and-Hyde performance had done another flip-flop. He was once more the charming man of the previous evening, and Kate was very relieved.

''Ah, now I feel a little more human,'' he said as he strode into the kitchen.

''I'm sorry if you didn't sleep very well.'' Her tone was apologetic, but Sam only laughed at her.

''I slept very well, considering. It's the waking-up part that's giving me trouble.''

''Then have a cup of coffee. There's a plate of eggs and toast keeping warm for you in the oven.''

She was just finishing up the last of her meal. But after Sam had seated himself across the table from her, she poured herself another cup of coffee and kept him company. Why was it that men always looked so good immediately after they'd showered, she wondered. Or was it just something about this particular man? Her gaze lingered on the faint sheen of moisture clinging to his skin. His lean cheeks were now free from the shadowy stubble, and his damp hair had been neatly combed.

"The roads are safe to travel now," she ventured.

He looked up from his plate and shrugged. "I figured they would be, but you're not really telling me something I want to hear, you know. I like being marooned with beautiful women."

"Sounds as if you've made a career of it," she said tartly. "And though I appreciate the compliment, I'm not exactly a beauty."

Mischievously he looked her up and down. "Maybe you're not Miss Dairy Queen, but you're not dog food, either."

Kate gasped a laugh. "Well, thanks a lot. Was that also a compliment?"

He nodded and leaned back in his chair. "I have a way with words, don't I? It's my Irish blood. Some ancestor of mine kicked the Blarney stone and broke his foot."

Kate sipped her coffee and gave him a considering look. "I'm curious. How did you happen to become a sportswriter?"

"It didn't 'happen.' It was shoved down my throat when I was too young to defend myself. My father was a sports freak."

Though there was a wry smile on his handsome face and he'd made the statement lightly, something told Kate that there was more here than Sam was letting on. It made her wonder about his childhood. She frequently found herself speculating a bit wistfully about the relationships people had with their parents. The intricacies of family dynamics struck her as endlessly fascinating. Maybe it was because she'd been orphaned so early in life, and Chris and Aunt Pam were the only family she had. Someday she hoped to have a family of her own, but so far it didn't look as if it was going to happen.

"Did you ever want to play sports professionally?" she asked.

"My father wanted me to. And for a while I wanted the same thing. But by the time I hit college I realized it wasn't going to work."

"Why not?"

He lifted a shoulder. "I wasn't quite good enough— not tall enough for basketball, not heavy enough for football and not fast enough for baseball."

As he spoke, he looked down into his coffee cup, his expression momentarily shadowed. Once more she was intrigued and wanted to know everything about him.

"You do play hockey," she pointed out.

Nodding, he drained his cup, put it down on the table and folded his arms across his chest. "Yes, but it's just for recreation. I'm not really mean enough for the game. To make it in professional hockey you need to have a well-honed killer instinct."

"And you don't?"

His smile flashed. "Nope. I'm a pussycat."

Kate was about to inquire into that statement when the phone rang. Pushing back her chair, she walked across the room and picked up the receiver. It was Chris.

"You okay this morning?" he wanted to know. "The weather was bad when I left the rink, but I didn't rea!

ize how icy the roads were last night until somebody told me this morning at work."

"I'm fine." Kate watched out of the corner of her eye as Sam got up to pour himself another cup of coffee. "The only thing wrong with me is that I ache all over from the cruel and unusual punishment of that workout you gave me," she joked.

As she finished speaking, Sam lifted the coffeepot and pointed at her empty cup. "Want a refill?"

Though he'd whispered the question, his masculine voice was resonant, and Chris had heard it. There was five seconds of silence on his end of the line, and then he asked, "Who's that?"

Kate's golden-brown eyes began to twinkle. Only the week before her little brother had warned her she was heading for spinsterhood because of her fussy tastes and prudish ideas. Maybe it wouldn't be such a bad thing for him to start wondering if she had a secret life.

"Oh, just a friend," she informed him airily. There was another long pause during which she knew he was dying to cross-examine her. But finally after merely clearing his throat, he just asked if she planned to make it tonight for practice.

"I can make it," she told him. "But I'm not sure I'll be much use to you."

"You'll work those kinks out," he assured her. After n exchange of quick goodbyes, the conversation was led.

ounds like that brother of yours is quite a slave
" Sam was leaning against the edge of the
eyeing her with a faint frown between his level

Kate picked up the cup he'd filled and nodded her agreement. "Chris has always been a perfectionist. He's really a very talented choreographer. But the routines he's worked out for us are tricky. I just hope I can live up to them."

"You don't sound all that enthusiastic."

"I have mixed feelings about it," she admitted. "I still love to skate, and I want to help Chris achieve his goals. But I'm just not sure about being a competitor again. It's a grind, you know. It takes a lot out of you."

"I know," Sam said sympathetically. As he spoke, his gaze lingered on her face, taking in the faint sprinkling of freckles across the bridge of her pert nose and the incredible thickness of her black lashes. They were so long that they cast shadows at the corners of her uptilted eyes.

He was surprised by the pure pleasure that just looking at her gave him. Last night as he'd lain wide awake in her living room, picturing her in bed just a few feet away, he'd wondered if the strong attraction he felt would seem like an illusion in the clear light of morning. It had happened before in the past few months. He'd meet a woman who seemed appealing, but when he got involved with her he'd realize that she wasn't what he wanted. Then breaking off the relationship would be painful. He didn't like hurting people whose only mistake was to bump into a lonely and therefore susceptible sportswriter. And so he'd promised himself he'd avoid that sort of situation.

But as he studied Kate, the attraction didn't seem illusory at all. He didn't think he'd felt this drawn to a female in a long time. The question now was what to do about it. Was he really ready for another involvement?

Very conscious of Sam's blue-eyed scrutiny and the feelings of sexual tension that were being rekindled by it, Kate looked down, focusing almost shyly on the tips of his strong fingers as they curled around the rim of his cup. "I suppose you'll want to be getting back pretty soon?"

"Yes. I have to check in at the office by noon. I'd better try that cab company again."

"Oh, no," Kate protested. Quickly lifting her eyes to his face again, she said, "I'll give you a ride."

As she waited for an answer, she almost held her breath. Somehow she sensed that a lot depended on his reply. The odd circumstances under which they'd met last night had made her nervous about being with him. But now her reactions were very different. At the moment there was no man in her life, and she'd been feeling a little isolated. She wanted to get to know Sam Ryder better.

He hesitated longer than was comfortable. But when he did respond, it was with a hearty "I'd appreciate that" and a smile that made her toes curl inside her sneakers.

"I'll just clean up here, and we can be on our way," she said.

He took her cup out of her hand, his fingers brushing lightly against her wrists. "I'll help you. I'm not much of a cook, but with a dishcloth I'm formidable."

TWENTY MINUTES LATER Sam followed Kate down the wooden staircase outside her apartment and then out onto Ellicott City's narrow, steeply pitched main street.

The sun had come out from behind the clouds, bathing the antique gray stone buildings with crystalline brightness. The ice had disappeared completely, and only an occasional damp spot next to the curb was evidence of last night's freeze.

Her hands jammed into the pockets of her padded jacket and her black leather bag swinging jauntily from her shoulder, Kate walked to her car. But when she glanced back she saw that Sam had once more paused before her storefront to peer in at the display. Turning, she recrossed the sidewalk and joined him.

"Why did you call your place Blithe Spirits?" he questioned.

"Oh, because practically everything I sell is old. Ghosts from the past, you know."

Sam chuckled and briefly touched her shoulder. "You're the imaginative type. I can tell by the way you've arranged those old-fashioned button shoes next to the silver tea service. Where do you get your wares?"

"Country auctions mostly. They're a lot of fun." It was on the tip of her tongue to ask of he'd like to join her next week when she'd be taking in a big estate sale. But she held the invitation back. Maybe other women could ask a man out for the first time. But not Kate. If Sam Ryder wanted to see her again after today, he'd have to make the first move.

A moment later she was glad she'd kept silent.

"I like old things, too," Sam volunteered. "Only in my case it's books. I didn't know that shop was here," he said, pointing to the quaint bookstore a few buildings down the street.

"Mr. Parker's place has been here for a long time. Almost all the stores here are closed on Monday, so it's not open today. But it's really a fun shop to browse in when you have some time."

"Hmm. Well then, I'll have to come back and take a look." As he spoke, he turned and walked over to the passenger side of the Volkswagen.

Searching in her purse for her car keys, Kate followed. He could easily have said "I'll come back to see you, and we can visit the bookstore together," she mused. But he hadn't. Did that mean she'd been imagining the attraction between them? Several of her girlfriends had complained about meeting interesting men at parties who behaved as if you were the woman of their dreams but who never called back. Maybe that was what would happen here.

The speculation made her tone of voice cool as she asked for directions. Sam seemed not to notice, and a few minutes later they were heading toward the Baltimore beltway.

Sam lived in a beautifully restored row house very close to downtown and the new Inner Harbor. Sportswriters must make good money, Kate thought as she pulled up in front. The formerly upper-crust neighborhood of houses with marble steps and graceful proportions had been declining into something like a slum a few years back. But a migration of urban professionals back into the downtown and a determined homesteading program by Baltimore's city government had produced a renaissance, and the wonderful old homes were once more sparkling and elegant. As she gazed up at the charming painted brick facade of the place where Sam resided, it was obvious to her that a lot of money and care had gone into fixing it up.

When Kate complimented him on the exterior of his house, he merely shrugged. "Actually I'll be moving out soon. I own it jointly with someone else who's left town and wants to sell out."

"Oh," Kate exclaimed sympathetically. "You must be pretty unhappy about that. Who is it? A colleague?"

"Something like that."

"Can't you buy their share?"

"I could," Sam said. "But I've decided not to."

Unable to take her eyes from the charming old structure, Kate slowly shook her head. "If I had a place like this to live in, you'd have to carry me out bodily to get me away from it."

"Maybe, but I think I'm ready for a change."

"What's it like inside?" Kate asked, too preoccupied to notice that though Sam had smiled, there hadn't been any humor in his eyes.

"Come on in and I'll show you around."

Kate was pleased by the invitation and looked up at him brightly when he walked around to open the door for her. As he led her up the stairs, she paused to admire the brass handrail and handsomely crafted knocker in the shape of an owl. Her praises were even more effusive once she was inside. Each room Sam led her through was more beautifully decorated than the last. But as she exclaimed over the exquisite furnishings and imaginative details that made the living room, dining room and kitchen special, she was more and more puzzled.

The house just didn't look like the sort of place a bachelor—much less a sportswriter cum hockey player—would have put together for himself. She couldn't imagine Sam Ryder lavishing the kind of care and attention that these rooms had seen. He just wasn't the type.

"Did a decorator do all this for you?" she asked, touching a finger to the pale gray herringbone pattern of the wallpaper above the chair rail in the dining room.

"You might say that," Sam returned noncommittally. "Come on into the study, and I'll show you my books."

Kate's brain was seething with questions as he ushered her out of the room. What had Sam meant? If a decorator hadn't done the place for him, then who was responsible? She was convinced that he hadn't selected the cut-velvet upholstery or the bergere chairs or put all that Staffordshire in the fragile looking lacquered curio cabinet. Indeed, in his blue jeans and down jacket, he seemed incongruous and even uncomfortable among the delicate textures and muted colors that prevailed throughout his home. Kate was pierced by a little stab of jealousy. A woman had picked out those things.

"You aren't married, are you?" she heard herself blurt.

He turned and stared at her. "No, I'm not. What makes you ask?"

"Oh, nothing. I just wondered."

"You are the cautious type, aren't you?" He shook his head and laughed. "No. Right now I'm as single as twin beds."

There were a lot of other questions she'd have liked to ask. But she didn't really think she knew Sam well enough to start cross-examining him about his private life. Undoubtedly there were other women. He was too

attractive for there not to be. How did she compare
with them, she wondered.

Kate was distracted from these thoughts when he
opened the door of a small study and pointed at the
bookcases that lined each wall. Now this was a room
that looked like him, Kate thought as she stepped forward and gazed approvingly at the worn but solid
looking leather easy chair and the overflowing surface
of the beat-up oak desk next to it. But the books in the
roughly built pine shelves were what really captured
her attention. They were mostly old, the sort of faintly
musty-smelling volumes one saw in rummage sales or
happened upon in an attic. As she knelt down to have
a closer look, she noted that there were some valuable
items among the junk and trivia.

"Oh, look at this," Kate exclaimed, pulling out a
volume with a faded red cloth cover and yellowed
pages. *The Book of Winter Sports*, published in 1912.
"It even has a chapter on figure skating," she went on,
flipping the pages quickly and stopping when she came
to a section titled Valsing on the Ice.

"Oh, listen to this," she said and started to read
aloud. " 'The valse is spreading wherever ice lies open
to the steel-shod foot of man or woman. Even on those
once jealously guarded preserves—the rinks of Anglo-
Swiss mountain resorts—the triumphant three-
step draws all within the sweep of its seductive
vortex....' " Kate laughed with delight. "This is mar-
velous!"

As she spoke, her eyes focusing eagerly on the print,
Sam leaned against the door frame. There was a quizzical expression on his face as he watched the way sunlight from the opposite window played over the planes

and curves of Kate's face. Gazing at her lips, which were turned up at the corners in a soft smile as she perused the pages of the book she'd discovered, he remembered how they had felt against his the night before. He'd been wanting to taste them again, but had held back all morning. An involvement with this woman wouldn't be casual, and he didn't want to start something that would cause either of them regret.

But she looked so sweet standing there with her cheeks flushed and her eyes sparkling. The temptation was too great.

Stepping forward into the room, he raised an arm, propped his hand against the bookcase behind her and looked over her shoulder at the page she held open. She glanced up at him, startled by his sudden nearness. But she didn't draw back, he noted with satisfaction.

"Keep the book if you like," he offered, touching her cheek lightly with his free hand.

Her beautiful copper eyes widened even farther, reminding him of a doe sniffing the wind and scenting danger. Perversely, her wary expression seemed to awaken the hunting instinct in him.

"Oh, no, I couldn't," she protested and started to replace the book on the shelf.

But he merely reached forward and closed his fingers around her smaller ones. "I insist. I really want you to have it."

"Well, thanks. That's awfully nice." Kate waited for him to release her hand. But he didn't. Instead he shifted around, turning to face her so that she was trapped between the lean length of his body and the wall of books. Still smiling at her, he opened her fingers and laid

The Book of Winter Sports down on the shelf next to her head.

"What would you do if I kissed you now?" he asked playfully.

Kate was gazing up into his dark blue eyes mutely, her mind taking in all the details of his face like a computer filing away information in nanoseconds. It was such a nice face, she thought a little dazedly. There was nothing about it that she didn't like. "I don't suppose it would do me much good to scream," she finally murmured.

"None at all."

"The neighbors hear a lot of female screams coming from your place?"

"Only screams of delight," he answered, lowering his mouth to hers. "So my advice is to submit cheerfully."

That was exactly what Kate found herself doing. When Sam's lips brushed hers and his hands curled around her shoulders to pull her closer, she leaned into him. She'd been wanting him to kiss her again. It didn't seem to matter that he was still a stranger and that she was alone with him in his house.

Last night there had seemed to be such a strong spark leaping between them. She had been puzzled and rather piqued by the withdrawn behavior she'd gotten from Sam this morning. But now as he held her close all that was forgotten.

At first the kiss was gentle and teasing, just as it had been earlier in her living room. But then it became more insistent. When he'd kissed her before, their bodies hadn't really touched. Now she was molded to him, her breasts flattened against his broad chest, her pelvis locked to his so that she could feel his hard thighs through the material of her jeans. Sam's hands were on her back, one at her waist while the other was curled around her nape. Kate's hands were resting lightly on the sides of his rib cage. But as he deepened the kiss, she moved them around to his back and then up to his neck where she touched with pleasure the short crisp hair growing there. As she breathed in, she inhaled the healthy masculine aroma of his skin along with the faint fragrance of the soap he'd showered with. Since it was her soap, she wondered if she smelled the same and if it was half as attractive on her as it was on him.

When he finally lifted his lips from Kate's and looked down into her dazed eyes, which had darkened to sherry, his own eyes crinkled at the corners. "That was fun, Ms Coleman. Want to try it again?"

"I don't think I'd better," she protested weakly.

There was a warm and sensuous glint in his eyes. "Oh, come on. Once was definitely not enough."

He was right, Kate thought as his lips again fused with hers. Abandoning herself to the pleasure of the kiss, she melted against him, waiting to see what would happen next.

She could feel his lean strength. It conjured up a vision of the way he'd looked naked, and as the image filled her mind she clasped him more tightly.

Sam's hands were not as stationary as hers. He moved his hands down her back to her waist, lingered there a moment and then shifted still farther down. In the next moment his tongue pushed past the yielding barrier of her lips to tease the inside of her mouth, and his hands slipped to her buttocks, cupping their roundness inside the tight jeans. Though he broke the kiss at last in order to nibble provocatively on the tip of her ear, his hands stayed put.

"I've been wanting to touch that round little tush of yours ever since I first saw you," he muttered into her hair.

Kate smiled and hid her face in the warmth of his sweater. "Well, now you have, so how is it?"

"It's great!" he growled, giving her a final squeeze and then tipping her face up to his. "You're walking around with some pretty fine female equipment. But you know that, don't you?"

Kate shook her head, but he only laughed at her.

"Sure you do. Women always know when they're pretty."

"Men do, too," she protested. "You know that you're attractive."

"Attractive enough to go out with me a week from Friday? I'd ask you for this weekend, but I've got to go to New York."

"I'd like to go out with you."

"Good. I can get some theater tickets from the critic at the paper. They're to a show at the Lyric," he went on, naming a Baltimore concert hall that was now a historic landmark. "It's a musical."

Kate nodded. "I'd love that, but I'll have to be at the rink for practice by eleven. So I'd better meet you somewhere in my car."

"You have to practice even on Friday?"

"We've got the ice rented for every night. The South Atlantics are only a few weeks away," she pointed out.

Sam looked momentarily irritated then shrugged. "It's a date, then." Kissing the tip of her nose, he lifted the book off the shelf and pressed it into her hands.

"How about meeting me here at six? Tony Cheng's is just around the corner. Since we won't have any time together after the show, we'll have dinner there beforehand."

THOUGH SHE LOOKED FORWARD to it for two weeks, Kate's date with Sam was not an unqualified success.

She made a lot of preparations, which even included buying copies of the *Globe* and scanning the sports pages for his byline. After reading several of his articles she found Sam was a good writer, sensitive and intelligent yet with a toughness in his prose style.

This discovery made her even more anxious to see him again, and she dressed carefully for the occasion. Though her silk shirtwaist was conservative and not particularly sexy, she thought its dusty shade of rose looked well with her gray polo coat. She was feeling pretty good when she set off for Baltimore late that afternoon.

As she pulled up to Sam's town house, she noticed a For Sale sign under the casement windows and shook her head. When he opened the door, she couldn't keep from remarking rather sadly on the sign out front.

"You really are serious about selling your castle. I can't believe it!"

Sam's welcoming smile faded. "Yes, I'm serious," he said brusquely. "Come on in."

Kate entered with a distinct feeling that she'd said something wrong. It seemed to her that there was a faint air of constraint about the before-dinner drink they shared in his beautifully decorated living room.

Later on their meal was pleasant enough. Tony Cheng's was a wonderful restaurant on Charles Street. Housed in a high-ceilinged old town house near the Walters Art Gallery, it was decorated in an art nouveau style that delighted Kate. The food was delicious, too.

But the company wasn't quite what she'd been hoping for. It wasn't that Sam didn't treat her nicely. He knew how to put a person at ease.

"You look like a winter rose in that dress," he said as he pulled out her chair.

Kate thought he looked pretty terrific in the charcoal-gray suit he wore, but she felt a little shy about saying so.

"How have you been doing?" he questioned when he'd settled in his own seat. "Any more bruises?"

Kate smiled. "None that I can't handle," she said and then hurried on when she realized the unintentional opening she'd created for his swift wit. "I've been doing fine. How about you? How was your trip to New York?"

Sam's wry smile disappeared, and suddenly he seemed to stiffen again. "Nothing that I couldn't handle," he muttered under his breath and then abruptly changed the subject. "Tell me about the skating," he insisted.

But Kate, wondering what it was about New York that disturbed him, shook her head. "No, tell me about your job."

He smiled faintly and began to talk about his work. An accomplished raconteur, he entertained her with amusing stories about his job at the paper and the sports celebrities he'd interviewed over the years. But again Kate sensed a certain remoteness in him, as if he were putting on a performance and waiting to see whether he meant it or not.

She didn't like being just an audience, and she didn't like his sudden inaccessibility. What was wrong with him, she wondered. Was he feeling guilty because he had another girlfriend someplace? Or hadn't he made up his mind yet about whether he really liked her?

All during the performance at the Lyric theater, the question rattled around in her mind. The play was the romantic musical comedy *Kismet*. As Kate listened to the lovesick Caliph belt out the line about being a stranger in paradise, she felt as if his words could be hers. Though she was intensely attracted to the man next to her, there was an uneasiness in their budding relationship. They might both be strangers in paradise, she reflected. She sensed that they were both reaching out toward each other but hadn't yet taken each other's hands. She was ready; why wasn't he?

The show was long. When it was over and Sam drove Kate back to his house, there was no time for her to do anything but get out of his car and into her own so she could make it to the rink by eleven.

"It was fun," Sam said as they were standing together on the curb after he'd helped her from the passenger seat. "But it would be a lot more fun if you could stick around."

Kate wondered if he meant it. The night was crisp and clear. Against the cloudless black sky the moon and stars stood out like bits of ice. There was a cutting wind, too. But as she searched Sam's shadowed features, she was oblivious to the cold. He was wearing a navy blue topcoat. A white silk scarf hung open at his throat. In the expensively cut formal clothing he looked very distinguished. The wayward lock of dark hair that the wind had whipped over his forehead only added to his appeal.

"I'm sorry I have to leave," she said. "I'd like to stick around, too." It was true. She'd have liked to go into that town house with Sam and let him kiss her again on that gray velvet couch she'd noticed in his living room. It didn't seem to matter that he'd probably kissed other women there.

A faint smile quirked his mouth, and she suspected he knew exactly what was going on in her mind. "Weren't you concerned about what would happen to your social life when you agreed to this ridiculous skating schedule of your brother's?" he asked.

Slowly Kate shook her head. "No. When I said I'd help Chris out, there really wasn't anyone I cared that much about seeing." She was aware that she'd made a pretty revealing statement. No woman likes to admit that she's dateless and available.

The admission seemed to touch something in Sam. He reached out and took her small cold fingers in his. "And now?"

"Now I'm sorry."

She waited a moment to see if he would kiss her. She hoped he would. Instead he squeezed her hand and then gently freed it. "Look, you'd better be going."

Kate's heart sank, but at his next words it slowly climbed back up into her rib cage.

"I'll call you. Maybe we can work something out."

"I'd like that." She unlocked the Volkswagen then and got in. Sam stood on the curb, watching her, a quizzical expression on his face. The wind whipped the fringes of his scarf, and he put his hands into his pockets. But it wasn't until she'd pulled away and glanced up into the rearview mirror that she saw him turn and go back into his house.

WHEN KATE ARRIVED at the rink fifteen minutes late, she was not in a good mood. As she swung her skate bag out of the trunk, she glared at the lighted marquee. If it weren't for her nightly commitment to this place, she would've been able to have a real date with Sam Ryder. What would have happened if she'd been able to spend the whole evening with him, she wondered. Maybe she'd never know.

On the drive from Sam's place her emotions had ricocheted between hope and irritation. On the one hand, he'd said he'd call. On the other, he hadn't exactly made it sound as if it were his prime goal in life. And that fact wasn't improving Kate's temper. She had a lot of pride, maybe too much for her own good. If a man didn't want her then she didn't want him. Except there was no way she could deny to herself that she hoped this particular man would try to see her again.

Chris, who was already in the rink, wasn't in a very good mood, either. Obviously he'd been skating around, checking on the clock every other minute and stewing because she hadn't shown up.

"Where have you been all this time?" he demanded when she finally skated out in her warm-up clothes.

"I was out on a date—a date I had to cut short to practice with you," Kate retorted coolly. Refusing to explain further, she started moving rapidly around the rink. Stiff from sitting for hours in a theater seat and from the irritable feelings churning inside her, she took a good ten minutes to loosen up before she rejoined Chris out on the middle of the ice.

He slanted her a puzzled glance. "Look, I can see you're in no mood to talk about it. But you're usually so dependable, Kate. Not showing up when you're supposed to just isn't like you. You know we haven't got much time. If we're going to succeed, we can't fool around. We have to be really dedicated."

"Well, maybe I'm not primed for all this dedication just now!"

The moment she took in her brother's reaction to her blurted words, she regretted having spoken them. He appeared almost stricken.

"Kate, what are you saying? You promised."

All her exasperation dwindled away. Chris was wearing his hurt puppy look, and she'd never been able to resist it. "I know and I'm sorry. I won't be late again, okay?"

"Okay."

He looked as if that wasn't what he really wanted to say, and the realization made Kate's expression soften even more. "This competition is awfully important to you, isn't it, Chris?"

He nodded in agreement. "More important than you know."

"Well, then, maybe you should tell me about it so I will know."

Chris hesitated, his gloved hands curling and uncurling by his sides. "Kate, when you quit competitive skating you were almost at the top. Yet you seemed to be able to just walk away from it and start a new life."

She nodded and waited for her brother to go on.

"Well, it was never that way for me." He shook his head ruefully. "I guess I must be just a dumb jock at heart. Since I left the sport, I've never really been satisfied with anything. Oh," he added quickly, "I'm doing okay with my job. But I need something else."

Considering his words, Kate didn't answer for a while. He wasn't really telling her anything that she hadn't already figured out. Chris was at some kind of turning point, and he required support. Who was there to give it to him, if not her?

Maybe it was because they'd been orphaned so early, but Kate and her younger brother had always been unusually close. Aunt Pam had done her best for them, but she was by nature a fussy and rather straitlaced woman with a variety of interests that occupied her to the exclusion of almost everything else. Though she'd provided a comfortable home and all the other necessities for the two young children she'd suddenly found herself landed with, she'd never been like a real parent. The result was that Kate had been more a mother than an older sister to Chris—always looking after him and coming to his rescue when he was in trouble. Now that protective instinct took over again. Chris had his heart set on placing in the South Atlantics. The least she could do was give it her best shot. It wasn't his fault that she'd lost enthusiasm for the project because she'd met a guy who interested her—or that the guy was playing hard to get.

"Okay," she said brightly. "What's on the schedule for tonight?"

"The lateral full twist in the syncopated part of the free dance," he informed her succinctly.

Despite her resolve to be a great partner, Kate couldn't stop herself from groaning. Chris had put together a very fast and challenging program. It was the nature of dance that the female team member took the most risks. Several moves had her scared. She could now do the backflip with a degree of security, but she found the full twist downright terrifying. One misstep, one split second out of sync when they were performing it at speed, and she could really be hurt.

"Now we're going to take it very slow until you feel confident," Chris assured her.

"'Slow' is the only way I can take it, so there isn't much choice."

Ignoring that, he put the music on and skated back to join her at their starting place. "You know perfectly well you can do anything you want to, Kate. You've always been a terrific athlete. It's just a matter of having confidence."

"I'm never going to feel confident about this."

"Trust me."

Kate laughed when she took in his earnest expression. "You've got the same look on your face that you had when you talked me into climbing old man Clark's trellis twelve years ago," she declared. "Now, I wonder why that's making me nervous?"

"Maybe it's because you fell off and broke your arm," he conceded, making a face. "But nothing like that is going to happen this time. I know exactly how to twist you."

"Easy for you to say. You're the twister, but I'm the twistee," she remarked dryly.

The tape clicked on, and Kate arched her back in the exaggerated posture that would begin the dance. An instant later the opening strains were blaring from the speakers overhead, and they started off in the quick complicated steps that began their routine.

Chris did a three turn and wrapped his arm around her waist for the first part of the maneuver. "Now just relax and let me do it all."

"Sure, sure. I'll just imagine that I'm a wet noodle with no bones that might possibly break."

"Come on, Kate! Don't talk like that. Think positive!" he said encouragingly.

"I am thinking positive—positively scared out of my everlovin' wits!"

AN HOUR AND A HALF LATER, Kate drove home with her eyelids at half-mast and a fresh collection of bruises on her body. After she parked in front of her store and dragged herself up the stairs to her apartment, she headed straight for the bathroom and ran a steaming bath.

I'd like to retire from active duty for a week or two, she thought as she slid her aching body down into the hot water. But that, of course, was impossible. Tomorrow was Saturday, and the weekend was her busiest time in the shop.

For long minutes she lay in the tub, her eyes closed and her mind an exhausted blank. It wasn't until she climbed out, wrapped herself in a fluffy towel and went to turn the light off in the living room that she thought again of Sam Ryder. What was he doing now, she wondered. Was he awake, thinking of her as she was of him? Or had he already gone to bed? A vivid image of his tousled head resting against a pillow sprang into her mind, and she grimaced at her own foolishness. Did it matter what he was doing? The real question was, would he call?

During the next two weeks Sam called several times. But to Kate's chagrin she had to put him off each time. Since she had no help, it was impossible for her to get away from the shop for lunch. And when he asked her to a basketball practice he was covering on Sunday morning, she had to beg off from that, too.

"Sunday is when the tourists visit Ellicott City, and that's when I make most of my sales," she explained.

There was a brief silence. "Just exactly when do you have free time?" he finally inquired.

The answer to that was almost never. Evenings were now out, and the only day she had free was Mondays. Unfortunately Sam's schedule was almost as complicated as hers, and he usually had to work Mondays.

"Well," he finally said after a not very warm-sounding chuckle. "Serves me right for wanting to take up with a busy lady. Give me credit for trying, anyway."

Kate stared down at the receiver in her hand as though it were an eviction notice. "Your team practices Sunday night, doesn't it?"

"Yes."

"Well, I'll at least catch a glimpse of you now and then."

The chuckle coming over the line was genuine now. "Possibly, but don't count on my being naked. Forewarned is forearmed."

Kate's cheeks turned a shade pinker. She'd forgotten how she and Sam had first met. "You're taking all the fun out of my Sunday night practice," she finally managed to joke.

After they'd exchanged one or two more empty pleasantries Sam rang off, and Kate was left listening to the monotonous buzz of the dead line. Scowling, she hung up and stood looking blankly out her little shop's display window. How could this have happened, she asked herself. She'd gone for years without meeting anyone who turned her on. And now, when it finally happened, she didn't have the time to find out if it was mutual.

"Damn," she muttered aloud. But there was no backing out of the agreement with Chris. She couldn't neglect her business, either. Nor could she really blame Sam for losing interest in her. What man wanted to treat a woman to dinner and the theater only to have her leave him standing in the middle of the street?

When the next Sunday night rolled around, Kate packed her sexiest skating dress and turned up at the rink early. Sam's team was still out on the ice as she walked in, so she stood at the Plexiglas window in the lobby and watched for a while. He had told her that he and his teammates just played for fun, but the activity below looked pretty serious. Even through the window she could hear shouts, muttered oaths and the clack of dueling hockey sticks. Helmeted players sheathed in padding crouched over their skates in the stance of warlike gorillas, careening off the boards and one another as they attempted to control the puck.

Kate tried to pick Sam out from the pack but was unable to. In their armor, the players on the ice all looked the same.

Glancing at her watch, she finally went into the ladies' room and changed into her own battle dress. Only, in her case, it covered less of her skin than usual. From her closet she had unearthed an old exhibition dress, a black costume with a low-cut bodice, high-cut briefs and a skirt of drifting petal-shaped chiffon. She had dozens of skating dresses, leftovers from her days as a competitor, but this one was special. It was an outfit she'd worn only once before, when she'd been eighteen and had skated to the strains of "Big Spender" in an amateur ice show. She remembered the occasion very well, because the enthusiastic response she'd gotten from the male portion of the audience had made her so uncomfortable that she hadn't worn the dress since.

Tonight, however, she was looking for a male reaction. Maybe it was undignified to resort to such tactics, but Sam Ryder wasn't going to walk out of here and forget her!

Stationing herself where she had a good view of the top of the steps, she waited for him to appear. Though embarrassed by some of the looks she got from his teammates when they began to straggle out, she held her ground. She was amply rewarded for her determination by the stunned expression on Sam's face when he finally emerged from the warming room.

He'd thought about Kate a lot during the week, wondering if he would run into her tonight and asking himself how he should handle it. He was interested in her, and he'd have liked to see her again. But what he needed was a woman and not a scheduling problem. If she were really interested in him, she'd make some time, he told himself as he trudged up the stairs, bumping his gear behind him. But then the vision on the other side of the cash register made him freeze in his tracks.

He'd thought before that Kate Coleman was pretty— cute and sexy even. But now he saw that she was gorgeous. She was wearing a black thing that clung to her curves and declared in no uncertain terms that she had a fantastic body. This was no girl: this was a woman, he realized with a little jolt.

"Hi, there," he finally managed to say. "You look great. That's some outfit!"

"I'm glad you like it."

"I love it! But if you wear it here again, you'd better pack a six-shooter. Some of my teammates have low temptation thresholds."

The statement was underlined by a chorus of wolf whistles as several more hockey players streamed past.

"Coming to JK's?" one of them called out.

"In a minute," Sam replied, waving a casual hand. Then he turned back to Kate, and his gaze lingered warmly on her. The black color of the dress suited her, he thought. It emphasized the rich ebony of her curls and the flickering golden lights in her eyes. When he said something of the kind, she looked pleased and at the same time secretly amused.

"My brother and I are trying to figure out what to wear for the competition next month," she explained, keeping her fingers crossed behind her back. "I thought I'd try this out on him."

"It's got my vote."

She grinned. "Thanks. Well, it was nice seeing you. But I better get out on the ice now and warm up."

"Sure." Sam watched her disappear down the steps and then stood indecisively in the lobby for a minute or two. Finally, almost in spite of himself, he wandered over to the window and looked out over the rink.

There she was, skimming over the ice like some winged fairy creature from another dimension. He'd almost forgotten what an incredible athlete she was. She made it look effortless, as though she were made of finer stuff than mere mortals and not bound by the same tiresome laws of gravity. Sweeping into a three turn, she did a series of high, graceful waltz jumps. Then she centered herself in another spin.

Arched backward so that her breasts were taut under the silky black fabric that barely covered them, Kate made an incredible picture—a dream of lithe feminine beauty, infinitely desirable and yet remote and unattainable out there on the empty ice. Turning away from the window with sudden decision, Sam picked up his gear and went back downstairs to the warming room.

Out in the middle of the rink Kate was beginning to feel irritated with herself and with Chris as well. This time he was the late one. She glanced up at the wall clock. Another fifteen minutes and he'd have her record for tardiness beat. Mentally composing the lecture she would deliver when he finally arrived, she began to stroke rapidly around the rink, going periodically into a series of fast mohawks and cross steps, which were part of the footwork she needed to perfect.

She had to keep moving fast or she'd freeze to death out here in this skimpy outfit. Had it done her any good to wear the stupid thing, she asked herself, looking down at the goose bumps on her arms and shoulders. She'd thought so when she'd spotted the look on Sam Ryder's face a few minutes earlier. But he hadn't exactly fallen on his knees and begged for another date. So maybe the whole thing had been in vain.

She was just skating toward the gate so that she could go out into the warming room and get a sweater from her bag, when the swinging doors opened and a man stepped out on the ice. She stopped in her tracks. It was Sam Ryder.

He was still wearing the jeans and navy blue sweater she'd seen him in last, but he'd put his hockey skates back on. Goose bumps forgotten, Kate stood with her hands on her hips, her mind racing.

As he glided toward her, Sam's hands were jammed in his pockets, and his expression was a little sheepish. "It looked like you were having so much fun out here, I thought I'd join you. If you don't want company, just say the word and I'll go away."

Kate was very quick with a denial. "I'm just goofing off while I wait for my brother. There's free ice if you've got the time to use it."

"I've got the time." He stopped a few feet away and grinned. His blue gaze skimmed over her shapely legs and focused for a few fleeting seconds on her feet. "I was watching you up there. You really move fast in those things."

Her glance followed the direction of his. "Figure skates?" Kate couldn't help getting a bit on the defensive. Traditionally, hockey players tended to look down on figure skaters and regarded them as sissies. "I bet I can cover ice as fast as you can on those," she challenged, pointing at Sam's hockey blades.

His smile widened, and his eyes began to sparkle wickedly. "Wanna race?"

Kate cocked her head and assumed a counterfeit air of belligerence. "Yeah."

"What's the prize going to be if I win? Better make it worth my while."

"You name it."

"I'll settle for a kiss."

Through her lashes Kate gazed at him sideways. "Okay. But what about me? What's my prize if I win?"

"Tell me what you have in mind, and if it isn't illegal or unhealthy, I'll probably agree to it."

"You left out 'immoral,'" Kate pointed out archly.

"So I did. But I'm a man of honor, so just say the word and I'll live up to my obligations."

She laughed at him. "I want you to let me teach you how to dance."

Sam was taken aback. But after a moment he shrugged and agreed.

When the bargain was struck, Kate selected a starting point for the race. "Three times around the perimeter?" she said, turning to him.

"You're on, little girl, but get ready to start puckering."

Kate's eyes danced. "Okay, Mr. Macho Man," she murmured, crouching slightly. "One, two, three—go!"

At first Sam was amused by the way she threw herself into the competition. This was one female who didn't do things by half measures, and it was pretty clear that she wasn't fond of losing, either. Kate was doing fast forward crosses to pick up speed as they rounded the first corner, and he wondered how that scrap of cloth she was wearing stayed up on her.

To tease her and put her off her pace, he shouted playfully, "Your dress is going to fall off!"

"Let it," she muttered between her teeth, not giving an inch.

As they began the second round, Sam began to sweat. This wasn't going to be any walkover. Kate Coleman not only looked fast, she *was* fast. If he was going to keep pace with her, he'd have to stretch. And he was beginning to see that beating her, which he had every intention of doing, meant that he'd really have to exert himself.

Grimly he set about doing that. But Kate was just as determined. Sam had been right in his assessment of her character. She'd been a world-class competitor in her teens, and she had the mentality of a winner. No matter who the opponent might be, in the heat of a contest she neither gave nor expected any quarter.

On the last round there were no jokes. As they dashed across the rink's glistening surface, both skaters were too much on their mettle to duel verbally. Bent low to the ground, Kate was at full stretch, a set expression on her face, her black curls flying. Though not as skillful as she, Sam was a solid skater, and his masculine strength gave him the edge. He finished a stroke in front of her. Then they both collapsed against the boards.

"My God, woman! You're a killer! Would you be interested in joining our hockey team?" he panted.

Kate giggled and shook her head, her breasts heaving under the scanty black outfit. "Listen," she said breathlessly. "You may have been a step ahead, but mine was the moral victory. I think you should let me teach you how to dance."

"You're right," Sam agreed. Turning so that his back was to the boards, he rested his weight on his elbows

and tipped his head back while he caught his breath.
His legs were stretched out loosely in front of him, and
the blades on his skates slanted inward. "But," he finally went on, "it's not going to be much fun for you to
try to teach me how to dance. I'm no good at it on my
feet, much less on skates."

"Why not?" she asked. "You're well-coordinated and
have a sense of timing. You ought to be a good dancer."

Sam shrugged. "I don't know. Too self-conscious, I
guess."

Kate looked around. "Well, I don't know what's
happened to my brother. But right now there's no one
here but us." She gestured at the empty ice. "Come on.
Who knows? You might even like it."

Sam doubted that. She was a better skater than he.
Nevertheless, when she took his hand and began to
show him some of the basic steps, he didn't pull away.

"The Dutch Waltz is the first dance everyone learns,
and it's very simple," she said, wrapping his arm
around her waist and demonstrating a swing roll.

Sam, a natural athlete, caught on quickly, and soon
they were gliding around the edge of the ice, grinning
at each other.

"It's a little weird without any music," Kate commented. "I think I'll put on a tape, and then we can try
The Swing Dance."

A few minutes later the strains of "Once in Love with
Amy" began to filter from the speakers. "Now," Kate
instructed, "just stand still while I do a three turn, and
then you glide forward while I glide backward—like
this."

Shaking his head good-humoredly, Sam complied,
and after a few false starts they began to circle the ice

together in formal dance position with the slow foxtrot accompanying them in the background.

"This is fun," he finally admitted. "But what if our blades get tangled up?"

"Then we crash in a heap on the ice. It happens all the time."

Sam's mischievous expression matched Kate's. "Maybe I wouldn't mind crashing in a heap with you," he murmured in her ear. "Though I can think of friendlier surfaces to do it on than the ice."

She looked up into his laughing face, entranced by the brightness of his aquamarine gaze. "Such as?"

"Such as a nice soft bed. You know that I've been wanting to make love with you from the moment we met. Speaking of which," he added roguishly, "since I won that race, don't you think it's time I got to claim my prize?"

Kate had turned a becoming shade of pink, but there was a smile curving her soft mouth. "I suppose that's only fair."

"Damn right," Sam muttered. Stopping abruptly, he pulled her against his chest and lowered his head to her upturned face. Though his lips were warm, his cheek was cool against hers, and Kate found herself taking an odd pleasure in the difference.

Sam's embrace was a mix of agreeable sensations. She could feel the nubby texture of his sweater against the bare skin of her arms and shoulders. She was pleasantly aware of the hard wall of his chest beneath the soft garment he wore and of the steel of his arms as he wound them around her back and held her to him. Their bodies were so close that his jean-clad legs rubbed against her tights, adding to the heady sensual mélange she was experiencing.

But it was the kiss that captured most of her attention. What was it about Sam Ryder's kisses that felt so good, so right? Kate didn't know, but as her lips clung to his, her eyes closed and she eased her hands around his waist then linked them tightly. She didn't want to let go. She wanted this moment to last forever.

It was not to be, though. Oblivious of their place and situation, they'd locked themselves together so closely that the accident Kate had jokingly described earlier actually happened. Unintentionally moving his foot, Sam caught her blade with his. Abruptly and without warning they were lying on the ice. Kate was sprawled on top of him, her semicovered breasts in his face.

When they got over their surprise, they started to laugh.

"This isn't so bad," Sam guffawed, enthusiastically kissing the V between her breasts where her neckline dipped. "Maybe I'd like it on the ice."

Kate started to laugh again, but sobered when she glanced up to find Chris staring down at them. She'd forgotten all about her brother, so it was a shock to see him standing there only a few feet away. Something in his expression made her painfully conscious of how odd she and the man beneath her must look. Scrambling off Sam, she got to her feet and tried to straighten her almost indecently twisted costume.

Sam, on the other hand, seemed in no hurry to get up. Looking amused and relaxed, he propped himself lazily on his elbows and glanced at Chris's face and then back again to Kate's.

"I'm late because of a blown tire," Chris explained tersely, turning toward Kate and ignoring her companion. "But I see you had no trouble finding yourself another partner."

"Only if we were skating to 'Send in the Clowns,'" Sam interjected. Finally he sat up and then got to his feet and started brushing tiny ice chips off his pants. Chris was shorter than Sam by an inch or two and, with his whipcord slimness, also slighter.

Kate made the introductions quickly. "Sam, this is my brother. Chris, this is Sam Ryder, a friend of mine."

"Happy to meet you," Sam said, sticking out his hand.

Chris shook it without enthusiasm. When Sam excused himself a few minutes later, Chris turned to his sister and raised his blond eyebrows.

"What were the two of you doing?"

"Oh, just kidding around," Kate said dismissively.

"It didn't look like that to me. Before you both got carried away and fell down, you were in a pretty passionate clinch with that guy."

Kate frowned. She'd been wondering how much Chris had seen. Apparently all, but so what? He was over twenty-one and did more than hold hands with girls himself.

"Yes, I was kissing Sam," she admitted coolly. "But I wouldn't have been if you'd been here on time."

The remark irritated Chris. "I told you I had a blowout. I couldn't help being late." His eyes swept her body, which was beginning to be covered with goose bumps now that she was standing still. "And why are you wearing a dress like that to work in?" He stared at it a moment, taking in the high-cut panties and plunging neckline.

"I wanted to show it to you. I thought you might like me to wear it for the free dance."

Chris looked even more puzzled. "But why? We already decided we were going to wear red. In fact, you were the one who insisted on it." Speculatively, his gaze skimmed over her torso, and Kate shifted her weight self-consciously. She really did want a sweater now. She was freezing.

"You were wearing it for that guy, weren't you?" Chris surmised suddenly. "And I bet I know why."

Kate's expression grew mutinous. She definitely didn't like the tone he was using. He sounded more like a preachy uncle than a little brother with his own set of peccadilloes to look out for.

"So what if I was?"

Chris made an exasperated noise. "Is Sam Ryder the man I heard in your apartment that morning when I called you?"

Kate didn't answer, but her face gave her away.

"He is, isn't he?" her brother demanded. "What's going on between the two of you? Are you having an affair with him, or what?"

Now Kate was really angry. "That's none of your business," she snapped.

"It is my business. You're my sister, and I'm worried about you." Scathingly, his gaze again panned over the dress she wore. "This isn't like you, Kate."

Her face had turned bright red. "You keep saying that, but maybe you'd better explain what you mean. What isn't like me?"

"One-night stands with guys you hardly know."

Despite the goose bumps on her arms and legs, Kate began to steam. "In the first place, my relationship with Sam Ryder is not a one-night stand. And in the second place, I do know him. He's a sportswriter for the *Globe*."

Chris looked unimpressed. "Big deal."

"What's it to you, anyway?" she demanded, thrusting out her chin belligerently.

All at once Chris's expression changed from one of accusation to one of concern. He stepped forward and put a hand on her shoulder. "I know what you think, but I'm not just being nosy. I'm worried about you, that's all. You're not acting like yourself. A guy like that..." He shook his head and then continued, "A guy like that has been around, Kate. You haven't, even though you're twenty-six. I'd just hate to see you go off the deep end and get hurt." He shook his blond head ruefully. "Believe me, I know because I've been there." He squeezed Kate's shoulder gently. "Just don't go rushing into anything."

She eyed him warily. But when she saw that he meant what he said and that he really was worried about her, she relented. "What do you mean, you've been there? Are you talking about Elise?"

"Maybe."

"Do you ever see her these days?"

Chris shook his head tightly. "No, but I heard she's practically engaged to some guy in accounting."

"That's tough, but maybe it's just as well." Kate hugged herself. "You know you're not sure what you want to do with yourself yet, and you're not ready for marriage. Maybe it's better that Elise found somebody else."

Chris looked unconvinced. "All right, if you say so. But why are we talking about me? You're the one I'm worried about. Promise me you'll watch your step."

"I'll watch my step."

He cocked his head in a question.

"Look, I really do promise. Just keep in mind that I'm a big girl and I'm three years older than you."

Chris laughed. "Sure," he said, putting his hands around her waist and picking her up as if she were a doll. "You're a big girl," he affirmed as he set her down on the other side of him. "Now run along, big girl, and get yourself a sweater, or you'll be a big frozen girl. You're turning blue before my very eyes."

5

ON THE LONG DRIVE home later that night, Kate had a lot to think about. Despite their late start, the practice with Chris had gone well, and she'd left with the feeling that their routines might actually be shaping up. She hoped so, as the regional competition was only two weeks off, and she now had a better sense of how much it meant to Chris.

As the Volkswagen approached the steep hill that fell away to the valley where her shop nestled, Kate's foot hit the brake. It didn't do to take that hill too fast. There was a sharp curve at the bottom, and a person never knew what surprises might be coming at the unwary. Just like tonight, Kate reflected. It had been one surprise after another. Her unexpected interlude with Sam had been delightful. But her tiff with Chris afterward had been a jolt.

Frowning slightly, Kate thought about that. She supposed it wasn't remarkable that he didn't like to find her kissing a stranger on the ice. It wasn't just that Chris had hurried into the rink in a bad mood because of his flat tire. He was depending on her to come through for him in this competition. Naturally he wouldn't be pleased with anybody or anything that might interfere with their success. Besides that, he was her brother, and he was concerned about her.

The frown on Kate's face disappeared. In the past it had usually been she who looked out for him. When they'd been growing up together, she'd defended him against neighborhood bullies, joined him in many of his boyish adventures and catered to his whims like an indulgent parent. In a sense they'd always been a team. But now it warmed her to realize that he cared enough about her to be worried about her love life.

Not that she had much of a love life, she decided wryly as her car rounded the corner safely and she approached the outskirts of town. She still had no idea whether she'd see Sam Ryder again. But she certainly hoped so, she thought, remembering his kiss. Maybe Chris was right and Sam was too experienced for her. But Kate considered taking his advice only for an instant and then shook her head. *I'm willing to take my chances,* she told herself. She was twenty-six, after all. Perhaps it was time she racked up some experience of her own.

Drawing up to the curb in front of her shop, Kate killed the engine and switched off the headlights. Sighing tiredly, she climbed out of the car, dragging her skate bag behind her. At this late hour on a cold November night, the steep, narrow street was deserted. Here and there faint reflections from the shop windows cast small puddles of light, but that somehow made the scene eerie. With its old-fashioned buildings from a bygone era, Ellicott City was quaint and charming in the daylight. At night it felt almost ghostly.

Shaking her head at the whimsical thought, Kate quickly began to climb the stairway at the side of her building. She was looking forward to the friendly warmth of her apartment. But when she was halfway up, her hand froze on the railing, and she drew in her breath sharply. There was a dark shadow at the top of the stairs. Somebody was lurking up there.

"Don't scream," a familiar baritone implored. "It's only your friendly neighborhood sportswriter."

"Sam!" she exclaimed, and her heart began to settle back into its normal resting place in her rib cage. "Is that you?"

"I think so, or I thought so ten minutes ago, anyway. Now my teeth are chattering so fast I'm not sure."

Laughing and forgetting how tired she was, Kate hurried up the rest of the staircase. "What are you doing here? You must be freezing."

"It's not warm at the top of your steps," he agreed. "How about inviting me in before I turn into Frosty the Snowman."

"Of course." Kate unlocked the door and pushed it open. "Tell me what you're doing here. I nearly had a heart attack when I saw you up there."

"You mean," he retorted, strolling in and watching as she closed the door behind her, "you weren't expecting me to show up here at two in the morning with a picnic?"

"A picnic?" Kate flicked on the light and then turned to stare at him. He was carrying two large grocery bags. "What have you got there?"

"Potato salad, roast beef and Dijon mustard, cheese, French bread, apples. I found an all-night supermarket near the rink. There was a liquor store next door," he added, setting the bags down on the floor and pulling out a small jug of California burgundy. "I hope you like your wine cheap and of recent vintage. The grapes for this were probably picked last month."

For a moment Kate was at a loss. Encountering Sam like this was the last thing she'd expected. Stepping forward, she peered into one of the bags. It really was stuffed with food. She glanced up at him. A quizzical expression hovered around his mouth, and she could see that he was waiting for her reaction.

"What on earth made you think of coming here at this hour of the night with bushels of food?"

"I don't know. I've been wanting to spend some time with you, and you've been awfully hard to pin down. But it was a pretty crazy idea, huh? You're probably tired. Shall I take my cheap wine and leave?"

Kate reached for the jug. "You shall not. Unhand that burgundy, Sam Ryder. I've just realized that I'm ravenous." She beamed up at him. "A picnic at two in the morning is exactly what I want. How did you guess?"

He grinned and began to unzip the brown leather bomber jacket he wore. Its mouton collar was turned up around his ears, which were still red from the cold. "You seem to be a lady with a mind of your own. I thought you might be game."

"Well, you were right." Now that she'd recovered from her initial surprise, Kate realized that she was delighted by this turn of events. She looked around her living room with sparkling eyes. "Where shall we have it?"

"We could go in your kitchen."

But Kate shook her head. "No, no. Picnics are meant to be eaten on the floor. I'll bring a blanket and some cups and plates out here."

Sam shrugged and smiled as she walked purposefully out of the room, her nicely rounded bottom in the snug jeans swaying pertly. He'd been telling the truth about wanting to spend some time with her. When he'd left the rink, he'd gone to JK's for a beer. But he was restless there, unable to concentrate on the conversation swirling around him. His mind was still on Kate, on the way she'd looked in that dress and the way she'd responded to his kiss. He'd wanted to see her again, but not next week or two weeks after that. He'd wanted to see her again right away.

When she came back she was smiling broadly, and she carried an army blanket and a pair of stemmed glasses. Setting the crystal down, she spread the blanket on the floor. As Sam watched her quick, neat movements, he thought how pretty she looked. She'd taken off her jacket, and she had on a dark red silk shirt that draped softly over her high breasts. Maybe she was too little and cute to be beautiful in the conventional sense, he mused, but there was a glow about her, a lovely elfin charm. And having seen her in that dress, he now knew she had a simply gorgeous body, small but perfect.

"Now, how's that?" she asked.

"Perfect." Sam picked up the glasses and then dropped lightly to his knees on the blanket. "I'll pour the wine and unpack the food."

"I'll bring plates, knives and forks, and then we'll be all set."

A few minutes later they toasted each other. Sam sat with his long legs stretched out and his back against the couch while Kate had arranged herself cross-legged opposite him.

"This is my first postmidnight picnic with a figure skater," he said. "I think we should drink to it."

"Good idea." She lifted her glass, and they clinked the two goblets.

"Do I gather from your silence on the subject that this isn't your first postmidnight picnic?" Sam queried as he tore off a piece of French bread and offered it to her along with the brie he'd brought.

She spread some cheese for herself and took a sip of the wine. "Actually, it isn't. I dated a guy in college who did something like this once. It wasn't half as good, though," she added quickly as she watched Sam deftly core and slice an apple into thin wedges. "It was just pizza."

"I suspect it's not the food but the company," he replied. He handed her a piece of fruit and watched her take it between her small white teeth. Irrationally he'd felt a stab of jealousy at the mention of this old boyfriend. Which, of course, was ridiculous. Kate was an exceptionally pretty woman. There were bound to have been lots of men in her life. But how many and how serious? And was anyone still in the picture now?

"Do you still see this guy from college?"

Kate shook her head and took another nibble of French bread.

"It wasn't anything important, then?"

Kate flushed slightly. The rosy glow in her cheeks was echoed by the brilliant color of her blouse.

"Well, we were engaged for a while," she admitted. She took another sip of wine and waited for Sam's reaction. Why was he questioning her like this, she wondered. Maybe it was a good sign that he was interested in her experiences with other men. Not that there was much to tell. She and Rod had been lovers briefly. But the experience hadn't exactly been the highlight of her life.

"Engaged?" Sam's eyebrows shot up, and he set down his wineglass in order to lean forward and look at her more closely. "Then it must have been pretty serious."

Kate unfolded her legs and shifted to a new position. "We weren't engaged for very long, only a month. And then I was the one who broke it off."

"Why was that?"

"Oh, I could just see that we weren't really right for each other."

Sam leaned back against the couch once more and studied her thoughtfully. "I had you pegged the first time, didn't I?"

Kate had pushed her empty plate aside and was tracing small circles with her finger on the blanket. But at his words her curly head jerked up. "What do you mean?"

"I mean that you're a very fussy lady. You want things just the way you want them—or not at all." If Sam hadn't been smiling, Kate might have been insulted. But there were deep brackets at the corners of his mouth. "Tell me, Ms Coleman, how many other hearts have you broken with your exacting specifications?"

Kate cocked her head, still not quite sure whether he was joking. "I'm no heartbreaker. I'm far too conservative for that. The truth is, I really didn't date much until college. I was so busy on the ice that I was socially retarded, I guess."

"And now?"

Kate's golden-brown eyes were candid between her thick black lashes. "I'm not a nun. I go out occasionally. But I don't date someone unless I really like him.

And to be honest, there aren't that many men I've come across that I do like that way."

Sam's gaze was steady, meeting and holding hers. "And how about me? Do you like me—that way?"

There was a breathless pause, and Kate could feel her heart thumping wildly in her chest. "Yes," she finally whispered. "That is, I think so."

"But you don't really know yet." His blue eyes were as bright as precious stones. "Well, neither do I. Maybe we should find out."

Deliberately he took her half-empty glass from her fingers and set it down on the edge of the table. Then, moving their plates to one side of the blanket, he drew her closer and grazed her lips lightly with his.

"I know you like me well enough for this. You do, don't you?"

"Yes," Kate admitted on a sigh. She leaned closer, wanting more of the brief, tantalizing caress. He'd been right in his assessment of her. She was careful about everything, including men. But when it came to Sam Ryder's kisses, she couldn't find anything to be choosy about. They were exactly what she wanted.

Her simple admission made him smile. "I'm glad," he whispered against her cheek. Then his mouth, this time warmer and more insistent, found hers again. Since it was so late, his chin was rather sandpapery. But she liked the slight roughness against her skin. That and the warm pressure of his mouth were bringing all her senses alive. Her hands crept up and curled around his shoulders, reveling in the hard muscle beneath his wool sweater.

He pulled away then so that he could look into her face. Her cheeks were deeply flushed, and her mouth had become a warmer pink from the pressure of his kiss. Feeling his scrutiny, her eyes snapped open. They were the color of simmering honey, he thought, unaware that to her his eyes were the matchless blue of perfect summer skies.

"I'm beginning to be pretty sure that I like you—that way. How about you?"

Kate didn't hesitate. "Yes."

"I'm glad you said that."

"Why? What did you think I might say?"

"Something like—I'll think about it and let you know tomorrow."

Kate shook her head. "I can let you know right now." She reached up and pressed her lips to his with a degree of enthusiasm that warmed his blood. One of his arms circled her waist while the other hand came up to cradle the back of her soft curls.

"Let's have another round," he suggested. "But let's get ourselves a little more comfortable so that we can really concentrate on this investigation."

"All right," Kate agreed. The next moment she found herself stretched out next to him on the blanket. Despite her compliance, little warnings were beginning to go off in Kate's head. If she wanted to sleep alone in her bed tonight, now was the time to extricate herself from Sam Ryder's embrace. But somehow the words wouldn't come, and she couldn't pull away. From the moment she'd laid eyes on this man, she'd been deeply drawn to him. Now here he was beside her, holding her in his arms and smiling so beguilingly into her dazed eyes that she felt her blood sing in her ears. She couldn't pull away. Not yet.

"You're a very kissable girl, did you know that?"

"What do you mean?"

"I mean that there are many parts of you I'd like to investigate closely."

"Such as?"

"Such as your ear." He nibbled on the lobe. "And eyelashes."

"My eyelashes!"

"Yes." Gently he kissed her eyelids shut and feathered his tongue along the line of her lashes.

Kate shivered and waited expectantly for what would come next.

"Then there's your nose."

"You can't be serious about my nose," she protested.

"Very serious. I think it's cute. I particularly like the freckles." He laid a playful kiss on either side of her nose. "Next there's your mouth." He stopped to brush her soft lips and then whispered, "That's just for starters. I think I'll save it for later and work on your jaw a bit."

"My jaw?"

He nodded solemnly, but his eyes were twinkling. "Your jaw and your throat are potent erogenous zones. Just relax now and let me have my fun."

"I don't know about you," Kate protested breathlessly.

"I'm thorough in my work, every little detail attended to and nothing left undone," he murmured as his mouth began to explore the sensitive line of her jaw and then moved down her throat. She shivered when she felt his tongue probe the beating hollow delicately. He had drawn her close to his body so that her legs were fitted against his. Her head was pillowed comfortably in the crook of his arm. His free hand rested on her

midriff, and she was vaguely aware that the chain cir-
cling his wrist made a glittering pattern of gold against
the ruby silk.

A minute later he slid open one of the blouse buttons. As she drifted in the dreamy pleasure his gentle
caresses were evoking, she realized that his fingers were
now touching her bare skin below the line of her bra.

She opened her eyes, but just then he moved back to
her mouth, silencing any possible protest with a kiss
that was different from the others—more heated, more
insistent. Kate felt her blood pound in her veins, and
when his tongue pushed past her teeth, she met it eagerly with her own. Unconsciously she had lifted her
hand to his hair, and her fingers twined excitedly in the
thick strands, then strayed to his ears and his neck as if
through touch she was trying to memorize their con-
tours.

His kisses tasted of wine, she thought. But that wasn't
the only reason they were so intoxicating. He knew how
to touch a woman. Compared to this artful seduction,
the other men she'd known had been bumblers. The
realization didn't lessen her pleasure. Her hands slipped
to his lean waist and held him tighter.

His eyes were very bright when he lifted his head and
looked down at her. "I was cold before, but I'm not
anymore. In fact," he murmured, "my temperature is
going up rapidly. Want to quit, Kate?"

"Do you?"

"No."

She looked at him steadily. "Then I don't, either."

"Good," he growled, as some of the tight control he'd
kept on himself slipped. "I want very much to see you."
As he spoke, his fingers went to the rest of the buttons

on her red silk blouse. A moment later it was open and sliding off her shoulders. His eyes darkened as he gazed down at her, and she was very glad that some blind feminine instinct had prompted her to wear special underwear. Instead of her usual sensible white cotton, she had on a sexy bra of beige lace. It was virtually transparent so that he could see her nipples through the lace as well as the swell of her breasts above the demicups.

"You're very beautiful," he whispered hoarsely. Now his manner was no longer so playful and restrained. When he undid the bra and pushed the lace aside, Kate knew that he was past the point of gallant teasing. His hips were pressed to hers, and through her jeans she could feel the hardness of him.

With most other men, Kate would have called a halt long before. But there was no thought of retreat in her head at this moment. She wanted Sam. It was absolutely clear in her mind. She wanted him.

When his lips closed over the hardened crest of a nipple, she heard herself moan with pleasure. And when he found the closure at her waistband, unsnapped it and slipped his hand beneath, she drew in her breath sharply. His lips were on her other breast now, teasing it to stiff excitement. Beyond thought of any false modesty, Kate arched her back so that he could take the swelling mound more fully into his mouth.

At length, Sam lifted his head and once more looked down. Kate was the picture of feminine abandon. Her head was thrown back, her cheeks glowed riotously, and her lips were parted.

"Kate, sweetheart," he whispered urgently, "listen to me."

Reluctantly she opened her eyes and gazed up at him.
"I want you tonight, very badly. But I have to be sure
you want me."

Slowly she took in the taut lines of his face. A dark
flush lay along his high cheekbones, and his irises were
fiercely blue. "Do you mean that you want to make love
with me?"

"Yes."

"That's what I want, too." She reached up to take his
head between her hands and to pull him gently back
toward her aching breasts. But he resisted.

"There's just one more question. I didn't bring anything with me tonight, and I won't do anything that we
both might regret. Can you take care of yourself?"

For a moment Kate was confused. But when she realized his meaning, she was touched by his consideration. "Yes," she answered simply. She didn't go on to
explain that she'd started taking the pill again only a few
days after meeting him. That admission would have
made her altogether too vulnerable.

"Then let me love you," he whispered gruffly before
he kissed her soundly on the mouth. "All of you!"

While she lay watching him, he began to take off the
rest of her clothes. The blouse and bra were slid completely from her shoulders and deposited on the couch.
Then his hands moved down to her jeans. "You've got
a sweet little body. I've been thinking about it a lot
lately. Did you know that?" he questioned, shooting her
a fast, hard grin.

Kate shook her head. "What have you been thinking
about it?"

"That I'd like to stop guessing and see all of you," he
said. He unzipped her jeans and then rolled the faded

blue fabric down over her hips. "I want to touch all of you," he added as he slipped the garment from her legs. "But first I want to satisfy my eyes."

For a long moment he did that. Under her jeans she wore nothing but a pale gold silk string bikini. That was the only thing covering her body. As Sam's intense gaze ranged from her naked breasts to her flat stomach and the small triangle of silk, his scrutiny heightened Kate's excitement. There was a glowing, burning sensation in her breasts and lower down beneath the fragile silk. If she had been able to think more rationally, she should have been surprised at the pleasure it gave her to have Sam look at her this way.

Slowly he bent down and touched his lips to a faint blue bruise on her hip. "My God, Kate," he whispered, "you're gorgeous. You need to be treated with tender loving care. It's a crime that you're letting yourself get knocked around this way."

"Bruises heal."

He shook his head. "I don't think you realize how special you are," he went on. "Most women look better with their clothes on. But not you—you're sensational."

"I want to see you, too," she told him.

"You will." Standing up, he quickly pulled his sweater over his head and unbuttoned his shirt. When that was discarded, his hands went to the snap on his jeans.

She'd seen him naked before, but that had been from the back and under such different circumstances. Now he stood facing her, unclothed. He certainly had no reason to be ashamed of his body, she noted. It was long, lean and very masculine with clearly defined muscles across his chest and along his rib cage. There was no hair on his chest, but it was dark and silky on his hard thighs and calves.

"Well?" he questioned.

"I wish I were an artist," she responded. "I'd like to model you in clay."

"You can model me with your hands now," he said, dropping down on the blanket. "I want you to touch me, Kate."

She did as he asked. A bit shyly at first, her hands tested the velvet and steel of his smooth chest and then dropped down to run along the rock-hard length of his thighs.

"That feels wonderful," he growled. Burying his lips in her throat, he guided her hands upward until they closed over his adamant masculinity. He groaned with pleasure, and his kisses grew hot and urgent. "Oh, Kate . . . Kate!"

Suddenly he pushed her arms aside and knelt beside her. Eagerly his hands tunneled beneath the silk panties that guarded the last secret of her femininity. Then, as his knowing fingers quickly found the sensitive spot that seemed to burst into flame at his touch, all the barriers were nearly down.

A moment later Sam had all but torn off the panties. When she was completely bare, he touched her again to test her warmth and then he parted her legs. Kneeling between them, he rested his head briefly on her stomach, stroking the satiny skin with his tongue and lips. Then he moved down, leaving a trail of kisses on the sensitive insides of her thighs. But that was only a preliminary. At last he found and persistently caressed the most sensitive place of all.

"Sam!" Kate exclaimed. She threaded her hands in his hair and twisted her legs as her overloaded senses seemed to detonate with pleasure. Awash in rapturous sensations, she felt her excitement building to flashpoint. Where had he learned to make love so beautifully?

When he was sure of her response, his lips were once more at her throat as he positioned himself above her. "Put your legs around me," he whispered, "and hold on tight."

She complied eagerly and gasped as she felt him thrust into her. Though he seemed to fill every inch, she levered her hips and pushed herself up against him harder to make this wonderful union even more complete.

"That's it," he murmured hoarsely. "Oh, Kate, we fit so perfectly. Let's go all the way together!"

She could only answer him with her hands and body as she clung to his broad back and flowed with his slow, surging movements. But he didn't seem to want any more words. The sweet communion they were experiencing was enough.

Already sensitized by his expert loveplay, Kate's body sang with each plunge. As a coil of excitement seemed to grip them both tighter and tighter and as Sam's pace increased with the building tension, Kate felt as if something were going to burst inside her. A moment later she was flooded with warmth and light.

With a shout Sam collapsed in her arms, breathing hard and gripping her shoulders. Then he took a deep breath, and as the thunder of his heart slowed he wrapped his long arms around Kate's waist. Slowly he rolled onto his back, carrying her with him so that she lay cradled on top of him.

"My God, woman," he whispered, nipping her ear gently, "you're a passionate little thing. You really had me there."

"Had you where?" she whispered back. Her eyes were still closed, and her cheek rested on his shoulder. She was still in a state of euphoric shock over what she'd experienced.

Sam chuckled. "Exactly where I wanted to be. What did you think?"

"What I think," she murmured playfully, "is that you've done this sort of thing before. You're awfully good at it." She raised her head and gazed at him. Between his half-closed lashes his sapphire eyes looked faintly amused.

"Thanks kid, you're not so bad yourself," he finally growled in a bad Humphrey Bogart imitation.

"All I did was lie there while you made me feel fantastic. You're the one who knew what he was doing."

She continued to look down at him, a question in her golden eyes. How many other women had he known? Was she something special to him or just one in a long line? The question hadn't really bothered her before. Now it did.

But he wasn't about to satisfy her curiosity. "Just seeing you lie there made me feel fantastic. Everyone is entitled to an area of expertise. In thirty years you have to learn something," he informed her with a cheeky grin. "And that's all I intend to say on the subject. How about another glass of wine?"

Kate shook her head. "Not for me, but you go ahead if you want one."

"Thanks. I think I will." Giving her an affectionate squeeze, he rolled her gently to one side. "One of the advantages of making love in the middle of a picnic is that you can easily take a break to fortify yourself for further amatory activity." As he spoke, he reached across to the jug and began to refill his glass.

Kate raised an eyebrow. "Is there going to be further amatory activity?"

Catching the expression on her face, Sam grinned. "Don't regard it as a threat but merely as a possibility for future consideration."

Laughing at him, she started to reach for her blouse, but he stayed her hand. "Please don't put that back on."

"Why not?"

"Because I like looking at you, Kate. Don't you realize what a beautiful sight you are to me?"

She blushed, and her eyelashes fluttered down. Did he mean that she was merely "beautiful" or "beautiful to him." There was a big difference. One was only a hollow compliment while the other might indicate something about his feelings. Kate was beginning to suspect that her own feelings toward this man were far more than mere sexual attraction.

Smiling at her sudden endearing fit of shyness, Sam stroked her shoulder and then the ivory slope of her breast.

"Actually," he whispered wickedly, "if you'll just stretch your lovely self out on the blanket again, I'd like to pour some wine in your navel and then lick it away."

Kate gave a little shriek of mock horror. "What? That's a terrible idea! Sticky and unsanitary!"

"Where's your sense of adventure? Try it, you'll like it." Sam's eyes sparkled with laughter, and he started to push her back down on the blanket.

Giggling, Kate batted at his hands. As a result, the wine Sam held was spilled not just in her belly button, but all over her torso, splattering her breasts, hips and even her thighs.

When she saw what had happened, Kate stared in dismay while Sam whooped. Then her laughter joined his, and she collapsed back on the blanket.

"Now I really have my work cut out for me!" Sam cried merrily. A moment later he'd dropped down beside her, and she felt his warm tongue laving away the droplets of burgundy clinging to the tips of her breasts.

"Oh, stop! You're tickling me."

"A man's work is never done. Hold still or I'll never make it to your thighs."

"Sam, you idiot!" Grabbing handfuls of his thick hair, she held him back. He leered at her impudently. Then they both fell in a heap on the blanket, rolling back and forth and laughing into each other's mouths between long kisses.

"If you won't accept the services of my tongue, lady, I think we're going to have to go into the bathroom and take a shower together." Sam started to stand up. "I draw the line at sleeping with sticky, unsanitary, wine-covered women."

"Oh, you do, do you?" Despite her breathless protest, she let him pull her to her feet. Their arms clasped around each other's waist, they walked down the hall to the bathroom where Sam ran a warm shower and washed Kate with loving thoroughness.

When he'd toweled her dry, he wrapped the fluffy terry cloth around both of them and pulled her close to his lean, naked body. "I don't want to go home. Will you let me stay here with you tonight?"

"Yes."

She nuzzled his chest. "I only have a single bed."

"All the better for keeping warm on a long winter's night."

Smiling up into his clear blue eyes, Kate tugged the towel from his hand and dropped it on the floor. Then she took his hand and led him across the hall to her small, old-fashioned bedroom. While he stood watching, she padded to her brass bed, pulled down the handmade quilt and climbed in. When she was under the sheet, she patted the mattress beside her and smiled through the shadows at Sam.

"Coming?"

"Yes."

In three quick strides he had joined her, and their bodies were pressed against each other, breast to hip.

"Kiss me, Kate," he whispered in her ear. "Kiss me like you really mean it."

6

THE NIGHT WAS a strange one. Sam fell asleep right away, but Kate was past exhaustion and her eyes stayed open. It was cold outside. Through the pane she could see the thin sickle of the frigid moon like a curved silver blade. Her old windows were far from airtight, and at times a wintry draft chilled her bare arm and shoulder outside the quilt. Beneath the cover, though, the heat of Sam's body next to hers warmed their bed.

Kate turned her head and looked at him. He had rolled away from her slightly, but his face was turned toward her on the pillow and his strong, regular features were clearly outlined in the moonlight. Though his body was no longer touching hers, her senses seemed still to be imprinted with its smooth hardness. Yet, for all that, he was a stranger—a man whom she knew little about. Chris had been right on that score.

As if trying to acquaint herself with Sam all over again, she studied his face intently. His eyes were so expressive that when they closed he looked subtly different. There was nothing soft or undefined about his features. His nose was straight and chiseled, his cheekbones angular. Despite the pleasure his lips had given her earlier that evening, his mouth was modeled along ascetic rather than sensual lines.

Sam had once described himself as a "pussycat." But Kate didn't think that was quite accurate. He was certainly a charmer. Hadn't he just charmed her flat onto her back? But she already knew that he could be moody and enigmatic. Now she suspected he could also be pretty tough. He wouldn't, for instance, hesitate to bid a lady a polite adieu if she no longer interested him.

Swallowing, Kate let her gaze drift down to his throat and shoulders, which were only partially covered by the quilt. She was vividly conscious that both their bodies were naked. And suddenly she was tempted to slip out of bed and put on one of her flannel nightgowns. Turning her head away, she smiled wryly up at the ceiling. What good would that do? It would probably look pretty dumb when they both woke up in the morning, and very likely he would tease her about it.

That thought raised another speculation. What *was* it going to be like in the morning? How would Sam behave? Neither of them had really been expecting what had happened. It wasn't as if they'd pledged their undying love or anything like that. Would he be embarrassed? Would she be?

For long minutes Kate lay awake, fretting about what might happen when daylight chased the silvery shadows from her room. But at last the demands of her body took over, and she closed her eyes and slept.

KATE HAD PICTURED the two of them waking up together naked and very close together in her narrow bed. That, however, wasn't quite the way the scenario played. At nine o'clock the next morning her phone started to ring. Jerked from a dreamless slumber, Kate looked wildly around the room and then, conscious of her nudity, tumbled from bed and rushed to the closet to pull on her bathrobe. Before running out to the living room to silence the phone, she cast a quick glance over her shoulder at the bed. Sam's unfocused blue eyes were open, but only just. Even as she watched, he closed them again and burrowed into the blankets as if he were a mole.

When Kate picked up the receiver out in the living room, the voice she heard on the other end of the line was her brother's.

"Sorry if I woke you up," he said.

"Oh, think nothing of it." She scanned the living-room floor and then put a hand to her forehead and sagged against the wall. In the morning light the blanket and the remains of last night's picnic didn't look particularly romantic. Clothing lay in tumbled heaps. The leftover French bread had undoubtedly gone stale. And there were red stains on the blanket where the wine had spilled.

This must be what they mean by the morning after the night before, Kate thought. She was having a little trouble concentrating on what Chris was saying. He was crowing about a new move he'd dreamed up for their free dance, and as he described its twists and turns, his voice was filled with excitement.

"What do you think?" he demanded.

"I don't know. It sounds like another sister-killer to me."

But Chris only laughed. "We'll work on it tonight."

"It's just two weeks before the regionals. I don't really think we have time to change the program," she protested.

"I know, I know. But you're good and you can do it. And we really need something special to impress those judges."

Sighing, Kate heard him out without really paying a lot of attention. She was relieved when he finally hung up. The beginning of a headache was starting to drill at her temples. No wonder, she thought, glancing at the school clock on the wall. She hadn't had much sleep. It had probably been four in the morning by the time she'd finally retired to bed with Sam.

The thought made her flush slightly. Drawing her robe tighter, she walked back toward the bedroom and peered through the open door. She'd been half expecting to see him sitting up in bed, splendid as a naked god and ready to seduce her all over again with a smile and a loverlike remark. But that was not the sight that greeted her. The beguiling lover of the previous night had pulled the quilt up around him and sprawled so that he now occupied the entire bed and gone back to sleep. All she could see above the edge of the comforter was a thatch of dark hair and an aquiline nose.

The corners of Kate's mouth tightened slightly. What should she do now? Despite her brief affair in college, she knew little of morning-after protocol. There was certainly no subtle way of slipping back between the sheets unobtrusively. It seemed to Kate that Sam should've been the one to wake up first and that he should now be devoting himself to calming whatever fears and insecurities she might have developed during the night. That didn't show any sign of happening.

After yanking open a drawer and pulling out clean underwear, she grabbed a fresh blouse and a pair of jeans from her closet. Then she stalked out into the hall, shutting the door behind her with an ungentle click. Dropping her things on the bathroom floor, she went back out into the living room and cleared away the remains of the "picnic." When that was done, she went once more to the bathroom where she quickly washed and dressed.

A few minutes later she came back out and stood for a moment, scrutinizing the closed bedroom door. Nothing stirred within. Apparently the man was still dead to the world.

Making no attempt to move quietly, she marched stiff-legged down the hall and into the kitchen where she set about making herself a large, comforting breakfast. She was just sitting down to eat when she heard a faint noise. A moment of silence followed, and then Sam's rather sandpapery sounding voice reached her in the kitchen.

"Kate?"

She paused with her fork between her mouth and her plate. "Yes?" she called back.

"I have a slight problem."

"What's that?"

"I smell coffee, and I'd like to come out and get some."

"Well, then, why don't you?"

"I can't find my clothes."

The lack of clothing certainly hadn't bothered him last night, Kate reflected. Aloud she said, "They're folded up on a chair in the living room."

"Thanks."

As she finished slicing her toast diagonally, she heard the sound of the shower running. Fifteen minutes after that Sam strolled into the kitchen. There was a scratch on his cheek where he'd cut himself shaving. His hair was wet, and his eyes were reddened, apparently from getting soap in them.

"Well, if it isn't Sleeping Beauty," Kate heard herself crack. Earlier she might have been shy and embarrassed. Now she just felt irritated and rather defensive. How did you behave with a man who'd explored every inch of you the night before?

Sam gave her a sheepish smile. "Sorry for taking over the bed that way. Morning isn't my best time. I'm not really human until I've had my second cup of coffee."

"So I've noticed. Well, the pot is full. Pour yourself some." She stood and took her plate to the sink, where she began scraping it industriously.

As he filled a mug, Sam eyed her small, rigid spine, and memories of last night washed over him. Who would have guessed that she'd be so sweetly responsive? He felt heat in his loins and wished she had stayed in bed so that he could make love to her again this morning. Why did she get up so early, he wondered. He tried to think back, but the hours after dawn were a blur. All he could remember was waking up to the smell of coffee.

"I suppose you're hungry." Kate's tone was cool.

"Some."

"Well, what would you like? I could scramble you some eggs. Or there are English muffins in the refrigerator."

She was speaking with her back to him as if he were a customer in her store—one she was not particularly interested in serving. When she'd finished, he put down the mug and crossed until he stood directly behind her. He put his hands on her shoulders and touched his lips to her temple.

"Kate, what's wrong?"

She went very still. "Nothing. Nothing's wrong."

"Oh, yes, there is. Is it something I did? Have I said something I shouldn't?"

"No."

Gently he turned her toward him. "Is it because of what happened last night?"

There was a long pause. "I'm not sure what happened last night." She refused to meet his gaze, and she was conscious of her heart thudding painfully against her ribs.

"Aren't you?" He studied her consideringly and then sighed. "Well, then I think I did something wrong. I got greedy and things went too fast, too soon."

She did look up then. "Is that how you feel about it?"

"How you feel about it is what's important. Tell me something. Are you worried that I don't think you're a nice girl anymore?"

Kate was well aware that he was teasing, but the question hit too close to the mark for her to be truly amused. "Oh, nothing so dumb as that. But . . ."

"Well, just to make sure we understand each other, I do think you're a nice girl, very nice." His mouth slid warmly down the side of her throat, and she shivered. He lifted his head and smiled at her. "But we don't really know each other very well yet, do we?" The smile turned into a grin. "I'm not speaking in the biblical sense, you understand."

She smiled back tentatively. "No, we don't."

"Well, it's not for lack of trying on my part. You're a hard lady to spend time with."

That was true, Kate conceded. It wasn't her fault, but neither was it Sam's. He wasn't to blame that she'd given herself so completely to him last night, when she hadn't really been ready to cope with all the emotional consequences. Indeed, she wasn't yet quite sure what all the emotional consequences were going to be. She only knew that at the time it had seemed right and she had wanted him very badly.

As he continued to gaze at her, he seemed to know what she was thinking. "I have an idea," he said. "Monday is your day off, isn't it?"

"Yes." She had been planning on taking inventory downstairs, but she didn't mention that. "It isn't your free day, though, is it?"

"It is as of now. I have an interview at five o'clock that I can't get out of. But I can play hooky until then. Will you spend the afternoon with me?"

Kate looked down at her hands. "Yes," she said shyly. "I'd like to."

After that the whole tenor of the morning changed. She fixed his breakfast and then sat watching him eat it. When she thought he wasn't looking, she stared at him hungrily, trying to connect the cheerful, good-looking man across the table with the skilled and passionate lover of the previous night.

They talked of many things, most of them inconsequential. She queried him on his work, and he asked her questions about her shop and her skating. She answered as best she could, but all the while, as she sipped her second cup of coffee and talked, she kept noticing things about him: the long fingers that had touched her so sensitively; the curve of his chin that she'd felt against her ribs when his mouth had caressed her breasts; the clean line of his throat where she'd seen a pulse beat so strongly. He had been the same man last night—the same, yet totally different. Though their conversation was as relaxed and casual as it had been before they'd made love, that fact changed everything. There was a resonance between them that was entirely new.

When breakfast was over and they'd cleared the dishes, he asked her what she'd like to do.

"I don't know. I didn't have any special plans for the day."

"I didn't, either," he lied. There was, in fact, an awe-inspiring pile of work on his desk. "But I have a suggestion. How long has it been since you poked around downtown or visited the Inner Harbor?"

"I don't know. A long while, I guess. I don't spend much time in Baltimore anymore."

"Then it's high time you visited 'Charm City,'" he joked, pronouncing the PR phrase with a wicked inflection.

A decade earlier Baltimore had been a prime example of urban decay. But as Sam's Toyota flew into the city's pulsing heart later that morning, signs of restoration and new construction were everywhere. Historic buildings were being refurbished, and towering glass-and-steel structures created a new skyline around landmarks from previous centuries. Parts of the city really were charming.

The centerpiece of this renaissance was unquestionably Baltimore's renovated Inner Harbor. Formerly rundown and abandoned, it was now one of the showplaces of the East Coast.

"Do you know your way around here?" Sam asked. He'd parked in a high-rise garage across the street, and they were walking across a pedestrian bridge that led to the Light Street pavilion.

"No," she answered his question. "I don't really get into the city that often."

"With your commitments I imagine it's difficult to get anyplace."

She nodded. But since her tight schedule was beginning to be a sore point between them, she refrained from commenting. She wanted to enjoy this stolen afternoon with Sam. She'd had such mixed feelings this morning. It wasn't that she regretted their love-making. How could she regret something that had been so wonderful? It was just that she wasn't sure what, if anything, came next. But now she was determined to ignore her uncertainties and make the best of her brief time with him.

"Well, if you don't come here often," Sam was saying, "then you probably haven't seen much of the aquarium."

"I've never been there."

"You haven't?" He stopped and gave her a look of mock accusation. "Well, then, we'll have to remedy the situation, Ms Coleman. Let's walk over that way now."

Despite the crisp winter chill in the air, it was a fine day. The sky was bright and clear, and the sun sparkled down on the water hemmed in by the wide brick promenades in front of the pavilions. In summer the harbor would be jammed with sailboats and rented pedal craft. Even now there were a few yachts tied up on the finger piers. One of the harbor's permanent fixtures, the historic USS *Constellation*, was still there for visitors to tour.

And there *were* sightseers. Even in winter, workers from nearby offices came down to stroll along the promenades. They carried bag lunches or bought something from one of the food vendors in the Light Street pavilion.

As Kate ambled along at Sam's side, she gazed about her appreciatively. The feel of the winter sun on her cheeks was good. She liked the fresh tang of the water lapping against the pilings and the cry of the sea gulls. They fluttered in the air like dropped handkerchiefs in a high wind and then landed to strut about and be fed and admired by passersby. Kate smiled when she saw an old woman whose thin legs were encased in argyle knee socks talk to the birds lovingly and toss out bits of bread from a huge shopping bag.

"Her name is Sal, 'the gull lady,'" Sam whispered in Kate's ear.

"How do you know?"

"I don't. That's just what I call her. She's here all the time, and the scavengers come to her like pets. I think she's given up on people and decided she prefers the company of sea gulls."

"Maybe there's something in that." Kate glanced up at his profile curiously. "I gather you're at the harbor fairly often."

He shrugged. "I like it here. I can walk down on a Sunday morning and buy croissants and coffee."

"You'll miss it when you sell your place and have to move," she guessed out loud.

He shrugged again. "It's already sold."

"So soon?" Kate was startled and stopped to look at him closely. In the past he had seemed oddly sensitive on the subject.

But now he returned her inspection impassively. "It was a nice town house. I figured that once the sign was up it would go fast. My only problem now is finding myself another place. I have to be out by the end of January." He took her hand. "Come on. I want to show you the seals."

They had rounded the north end of the promenade and were now on the other side of the World Trade Center. The new aquarium had angular lines and an off-center pyramidal roof and was built on the end of a concrete pier that jutted out at right angles to the pavilions across the water.

"This is the best time to visit this place," Sam was saying. "On weekends people are lined up to get in, and you can't see the exhibits for the crowds."

He didn't, however, take her to the escalator that snaked up to the second-story entrance. Instead, he led her past it and around a concrete support to a large outdoor pool. It, too, was formed from concrete. In the center of it were large rocks and a rough shelf shaped from the same material.

"Oh, there really are seals," Kate exclaimed, peering over the top of the slatted iron rail that rimmed the enclosure.

Sam grinned down at her dark head indulgently. "I told you."

The creatures were cruising underwater on their backs, sleek fat shapes that were utterly graceful in the element that was so obviously their home. Every now and then, one would poke a head out and eye the small group of five or six people that stood looking down. There were four seals: a bull and three smaller females.

"His name is Ike," Sam explained when the big male crawled up onto the shelf to sun himself.

"Did you make that up, too?"

"No, that really is his name. The females are Orange, Apples and Peaches." Sam winked. "Ike likes fruit cocktail."

Kate's cheeks were already ruddy from the chill wind blowing off the water, but they deepened a shade. "I see." She glanced down at the plaque affixed to the cement wall. "It says here that gray seals are polygamous and keep a harem of a dozen or so females, but that harbor seals are monogamous. Which is Ike?"

Sam looked quizzical. "The evidence suggests he likes his ladies in the plural."

"I guess so." Kate gazed down at the pool, but she wasn't really thinking about the big seal lounging there at his ease. She was thinking about Sam. How did he like his ladies? Had she just joined an informal harem? The notion was so repugnant to her that she shivered inside her down jacket. Again she was painfully conscious of how little she knew about this man. Knowing far less about him than she would about someone she'd hire in her shop, she'd let him become her lover. She'd told him about her one and only serious love affair, but she had no idea if he was currently involved with another woman.

"You look cold," Sam said. "Why don't we go in? It's warm in there. On the top floor they even have a tropical rain forest complete with parrots."

Once more he took her hand, and despite all her doubts her fingers laced into his trustingly. It seemed to be a natural response that had no connection with logic.

The aquarium's central core was a spiraling glass-covered waterway where sharks and large game fish circled lazily. As Kate watched in fascination, a giant ray glided sinuously past like some strange evil angel.

The rest of the building was interesting as well. On the next level there was a sea-cliff exhibit where they saw a puffin dive into a pond and swim underwater. A coral reef display reproduced the clear sunlit waters of the Pacific. There was even a children's cove where you could reach in and examine various kinds of crabs, starfish and sea urchins.

Kate and Sam stopped in a small nearby theater to watch a beautiful eight-minute film about water sounds. The star attraction, of course, was the song of the humpback whale.

"Why do you suppose they sing?" Kate whispered.

"Everyone sings in the bathtub," Sam teased gently and squeezed her hand. "Don't you?"

"No," she denied a little too quickly.

There was an amused glimmer between Sam's long lashes. "I don't believe you. But I'll just have to see for myself, won't I?"

She shot him a look and then laughed at his guileless expression. "I don't think so."

"No? I'll have to see if I can change your tune on that."

That was the trouble, Kate thought, glancing away quickly. He probably could. She certainly hadn't had much luck resisting Sam Ryder so far.

When they finally left the aquarium, it was well into the afternoon. "Hungry?" he asked. He glanced at his watch. "You made such a good breakfast that I didn't even think about lunch. But I could eat something now."

Kate agreed to that, and side by side they headed back toward the Light Street pavilion. It housed a colorful food market as well as numerous restaurants. Kate thought that Sam might just want to buy something from one of the stands. But when she asked, he shook his head.

"No, let's find a restaurant where we can sit down and be comfortable. There's a place called the Soup Kitchen. How does that sound?"

It sounded great. The sky had become overcast, and after the aquarium's almost tropical warmth the wind felt particularly sharp. A bowl of hot soup would be the perfect antidote.

The Soup Kitchen was downstairs in the pavilion and looked out on the harbor. Since the place was less than half-full at this time in the afternoon, Sam and Kate were quickly shown to a table by the window.

Kate looked around approvingly at the restaurant's natural woodwork, shiny tile floors and colorful burgundy-and-white tablecloths. Then she picked up her menu and studied it.

Sam glanced over at her inquiringly. "What are you going to have?"

"The cream of broccoli soup sounds good."

"It sounds terrible to me, but I won't stand in your path." He threw down his menu. "I'll settle for a roast-beef sandwich. Since this is a special occasion, shall we celebrate with a glass of wine?"

"What sort of special occasion is it?" Kate's eyes met his frankly.

Sam's lips quirked at the corners. "Don't you re-member? We're finally getting to know each other."

The waitress came just then to take their order, and Sam gestured toward Kate. "The lady would like to start with a glass of wine."

"Chablis," Kate quickly supplied.

Sam requested a bottle of Canadian ale for himself. When the girl left, he slanted Kate an amused look. "You've lost your taste for cheap burgundy, I see."

She gaped at him and then swallowed. Though it seemed incredible, she'd momentarily forgotten last night's wine episode. Now color stormed to her cheeks as she recalled how his tongue had laved the spilled dark red droplets from her naked breasts.

"Sam," she suddenly blurted, "I have to ask you something."

"Ask away."

She clasped her hands together, wondering how she was going to put this. "Am I...that is...are you seeing many other women?"

He was silent for a moment, and she fleetingly got the impression that his azure eyes had taken on a secretive cast. "There's no one special in my life at the moment."

She relaxed, but not altogether happily. Did that statement include her, she wondered. It wasn't that she wanted a declaration of undying love. She wasn't yet ready to make such a commitment herself. Yet, despite that, she wanted him to reassure her—to tell her that *their* lovemaking *had* been special.

"I'm very attracted to you, Kate."

"What?" She stared at him, wondering if he were a mind reader.

"Obviously, after last night, you must know that. What I'm saying is that as far as I'm concerned it wasn't just a fluke or a one-night stand. The thing is, like you, I'm not just exactly sure what it was." He reached across and grasped her hand. "Let's not waste our time worrying about it or analyzing it. Let's just relax and see where it goes from here."

The waitress brought their drinks then. When she'd gone, Sam said, "I have to go out of town to cover some games and to take care of some personal matters, but I'll phone you when I get back from New York."

Kate sipped at her wine, not really tasting it because her brain was racing. "You must be very busy right now. Didn't you say that you had to move out of your house in January?"

"Yes, I have to start looking around for another place." He shot her a lopsided grin. "I'd invite you to look with me, but I don't suppose you could find the time."

Kate nodded reluctantly. She'd love to go apartment hunting with him. "I'm afraid not. Not until the regionals are over, anyhow."

"What happens after that?" Sam's eyes narrowed slightly.

"If we don't at least come in third, nothing." That was the deal she'd made with Chris when he'd first talked her into this thing. If they didn't place, they would stop working together. Should he want to try again next year, he'd have to look around for another partner. Of course, it had seemed like a lark then, and she hadn't realized how committed her brother was going to be to the whole thing. Maybe she should remind Chris of their original agreement, just to be sure he hadn't forgotten.

"And if you do place?" Sam interrupted her thoughts.

"Then we'll go on to Easterns."

"After that?"

While their meals were set in front of them, Kate gazed back at him silently. "Well, I haven't really thought about that," she said at last. "Frankly, I'll be surprised if we even get past the regionals."

"Why? You and your brother are both good skaters." He looked meditatively down at his roast-beef sandwich. "Are you up against a lot of competition?"

"Well, actually, no," Kate conceded. She spooned up some soup. It was hot and delicious.

"How many will be lined up against you?"

"There are only six other couples that I know of."

"Six!" Sam's dark eyebrows flew up. "Then it sounds to me like your odds are excellent."

"That's one of the reasons why Chris was so keen to do it this year," she said. "He thought we had a good chance."

"I agree with him." Sam twirled his glass between his fingers, causing the inch or two of ale left in it to slosh like a miniature storm-tossed sea. "Will you be practicing just as hard if you go on to the Easterns?"

"Harder," Kate mumbled. She put down her spoon. Suddenly the soup didn't taste so good.

"Harder!"

"The competition will be tougher there. We'd really have to be at our best so as not to make a poor showing," she explained defensively. "Even if you don't expect to win, you don't want to look bad, either."

Sam's sapphire eyes pinned her. "What happens if you do win there?"

"We'd have to start preparing for the nationals." Kate pushed her half-full bowl away. She was beginning to feel like the victim of an inquisition. And Sam was starting to look the part, she thought, glancing up at him. His face was set in stern lines and his eyes had lost all their warmth.

"What will that mean?"

"Constant practice." The two words didn't begin to tell the whole story. She knew because she'd once been a national competitor. To stay on top at that level meant living and breathing the ice. You could think of nothing else. It dominated your life entirely.

Kate threw up her hands. "I know what you're thinking. But honestly, Sam, that's not going to happen. You have no idea how exacting the competition is at that level. I just don't think Chris and I will make it that far. For one thing, we haven't been dancers long enough."

"But you must have thought you had a chance when you agreed to do it," Sam insisted.

She shook her head emphatically. "I said yes to it only because I felt Chris needed my help, and I just couldn't turn him down." Unconsciously she laced her fingers together. "I hadn't met you then. I already told you, there was no one I was particularly interested in. Giving up my evenings wasn't a terrible sacrifice. When Chris suggested we team up, it didn't seem like such a bad idea. It's not as if I don't like to skate. I love it, and I enjoy being with him. We always have a lot of fun together. How could I know that it would turn into such a—"

"Such a hassle?" Sam regarded her levelly. "Well, you have met me now, and I'd like to spend time with you. Couldn't you cut down on your practice schedule a little? How could staying away from that rink one evening a week make a big difference?"

Kate shook her head again. "I can't. Not with the South Atlantics so close. I just couldn't do that to Chris. You have to understand about my brother. Skating was all he ever really wanted to do. And when he didn't make it to the top, he was crushed. I think that in the years since then he's been trying to find himself, but never really has."

"If skating's so important to him, why doesn't he teach it?"

"He's never wanted to teach. He wants to skate. They're two very different things."

Sam's voice was gruff. "All right, then, why doesn't he try again on his own? Why does he have to involve you?"

"At twenty-three he's too old to go anywhere as a singles competitor. But he's not too old for dance. And he's really good at it. Honestly, I think he's finally found his niche. But for dance you need a partner."

Sam folded his arms across his chest and eyed her. "How about you? Does that mean you've found your niche, too?"

"Oh, no!" Kate was so quick with her denial that her voice sounded breathless. "I'm happy with my life the way it is. I don't want to be a competitor again. I'm getting too old for it, anyway."

His mouth softened slightly. "Over the hill at twenty-six?"

"Yes, for amateur competitive figure skating, at any rate."

"But if your brother is ambitious, I don't suppose he intends to stay an amateur." Sam's face was reflective. "If you make it at the national level, you could then command a lot of money as professionals, couldn't you?"

"Yes," Kate admitted reluctantly.

"That's what your brother is after, isn't it?"

"I don't think so. We haven't really discussed it that far." But as she spoke, Kate realized she was deceiving herself. True, Chris had never actually said he wanted to quit his computer job and skate professionally. But very likely that was precisely what he yearned for. Given the amount of work he was putting into this effort, it was the only thing that made sense.

"Of course that's what he wants," Sam stated unequivocally. "He's not crazy. He's ambitious for something, and he's going for it. Well, I can't blame him for that. In fact I admire him. What I'm curious about is why you're going with him."

Battered by Sam's relentless cross-examination, Kate scrutinized him mutinously. She wasn't about to admit that she'd just realized he was right.

"I told you. I'm just trying to help Chris out. That's all there is to it. I don't want to be a skating professional. It would mean constant travel, a grueling schedule. I'd have to sell my shop." She shook her head emphatically. "That's not for me."

Sam looked maddeningly unconvinced. "You're exhausting yourself, ruining your social life, risking your bones and coming home in the wee hours of the morn-

ing covered with bruises, yet you don't share any of
your brother's ambitions?"

Put like that, it did sound a little bizarre, Kate acknowledged. In fact, she was just beginning to realize
how bizarre this whole situation was becoming. But
again, she wasn't going to admit that to him. "It's just
until the regionals."

"Maybe. Maybe not." Abruptly, Sam signaled for the
check and then reached into his back pocket for his
wallet. "It's my opinion that you've allowed yourself
to be talked into a roller-coaster ride. When it starts
picking up speed you may not be able to get off, even
if you want to."

Kate watched him rebelliously, half angry, half distressed by what he was saying. "So what do you think
I should do?"

"If you're being honest about not wanting any of this,
you should level with your brother. I don't think the
poor guy knows how you feel." He laid several bills on
the table, glanced at his watch and stood up. "It's later
than I realized. I'm going to have to put you in a cab if
I'm to make my appointment."

Kate's mind was still dwelling on his first statement.
She pushed back her chair and rose to her feet. "I
couldn't possibly back out on Chris at this point. That
would be a terrible thing to do."

He took her arm and led her out of the restaurant.
"There are worse things than allowing his ambitions to
ruin your life."

"They're not ruining my life. And anyway, it's just
until the—"

"I know, I know, it's just until the regionals!"

Sam sounded cynical, and Kate was so angry and upset that she couldn't bring herself to utter another word. In stiff silence they walked side by side out of the pavilion and into the wintry air. The clouds hanging in the sky were now thick and gray, and the wind cut like a knife. Kate jammed her hands into her pockets and watched while Sam flipped up his collar. She could feel angry tears at the back of her eyes and wondered if she could believe what he'd told her earlier—that he would call. Maybe this was the last time she would see him.

"There are usually taxis on that corner," he said, taking her arm.

He was right. It was only a minute or two before he'd successfully hailed a cab. It was going in the opposite direction. While they waited for it to turn around and head back, Sam turned toward Kate and grasped her shoulders.

"You're mad at me because of what I said, aren't you?"

"No, of course not," she muttered.

"Sure you are. You look as if you'd like to kick me. I wouldn't have said it, you know, if I didn't give a damn."

"What makes you think I give a damn?" She felt as cold as ice inside her jacket.

Sam's eyes searched hers. "Do you?"

"Yes," she hissed, her teeth chattering.

"Me, too." He lowered his head and kissed her hard and fast. Then he pushed open the door of the waiting cab and settled her inside.

"This lady wants to go to Ellicott City," he told the driver and handed the man money to cover the fare. When that was done, he gave Kate a brief salute then swiveled and walked away. Looking over her left shoulder, she watched his swiftly receding back until her cab turned the corner.

7

SAM DID CALL that weekend. But it was only to say he had to go out of town again. He was covering the Baltimore hockey team for a hospitalized colleague and had to accompany the team on road trips.

Kate was almost glad. If he'd asked her out, she wouldn't have been able to find the time. With the regionals coming up in a few days, she and Chris were practicing at a ferocious pace. She'd even had to hire temporary help in the shop because they were using the afternoons to work, besides the extra hours they picked up earlier in the evenings.

But even though she couldn't see Sam, she didn't stop thinking about him and their puzzling nonaffair. What, if anything, was happening between them, she wondered. Sam was on her mind constantly. And though she didn't hear from him often, some sixth sense told her he, also, was thinking about her.

Her preoccupation was noticeable even to others. "You're not concentrating," Chris complained one afternoon. "Honestly, Kate, you act sometimes like you're only half here."

Kate was instantly contrite. Once again she had been daydreaming about Sam. "Do you want to try that section of the dance over?" she offered.

"We'll have to. I know it's not the hardest part, but the timing has got to be perfect. You can't let your mind wander."

"I know, I know."

"Do you?" Chris's brown eyes searched hers. "Kate, everything depends on getting this absolutely right. Everything!"

The urgency in her brother's voice made Kate's shoulders droop slightly. Though somehow they hadn't found the time to sit down and have a discussion about his ambitions for the future, she knew he was pinning all his hopes on this competition. That meant he was counting on her to come through for him.

"Chris," she assured him in a low voice, "I'll be there when you need me. Now let's try that footwork again, and this time I promise it will be flawless."

Kate kept her pledge. By the end of that week all their routines were perfect with only an occasional bobble to keep them on their toes. As she drove home from the rink the night before she was to travel to Alexandria where the competition would be held, Kate felt confident that she and Chris would turn in at least a respectable performance. But that wasn't what she was thinking about when she climbed the stairs to her apartment. She was thinking of Sam.

He'd called her again earlier that week. After he'd casually asked how she was, he'd wanted to know if there was any time when they could have dinner. There hadn't been. She had to gulp down all her meals at the shopping center between practice sessions. It had just about killed her to turn him down.

"Well, nothing ventured, nothing gained," he'd retorted coolly. She'd had no trouble identifying the annoyance threading his lazy drawl. She couldn't blame him. But it wasn't her fault, either. Unless he wanted to stand around and freeze on her porch after midnight, there was no way they could see each other until the regionals were over.

The thought made her peer up into the shadows at the top of the landing, half hoping he might be there. But it was deserted. Sighing, Kate finished the climb, unlocked her door, stepped into the warmth of her living room and slung her skate bag down on the floor. She'd fallen again tonight, and she wondered if the costumes she'd be wearing tomorrow would cover the bruises. It wouldn't enhance the Colemans' performance if she went out on the ice in front of the judges looking as battered as she felt.

She had just taken off her jacket when she heard the phone ring. Thinking it might be Chris with some new stricture about tomorrow, she picked it up warily. But the resonant baritone at the other end of the line made her straighten.

"Hi. It's Sam. Did I wake you?"

"No, I just got in." She gripped the phone tighter. "It's nice to hear your voice."

"I like the sound of you, too. The sight would be even more welcome." He paused, and she tried to think of a clever retort. His next words made her forget the attempt. "I'm calling to warn you that you'll be running into me tomorrow."

"What?"

"I'm going to cover that competition for the sports page here at the *Globe*."

"How did you manage that?" Kate was amazed. Regional figure-skating competitions never made the newspapers. Even national ones were rarely featured. It was only on the Olympic level that a figure-skating champion could hope to be written up the way a local football or basketball hero might be.

"I talked my editor into it," Sam explained with a chuckle. "You'll have to help me out, though. I'll be there taking notes, but I'm not sure I'm going to understand what I see."

"I'll be glad to answer any questions you might have."

"Good. I'll hold you to it, then."

There wasn't much more to the conversation, but it was enough to buoy Kate's spirits. When she'd hung up the phone, she sat down on the couch and stared at the place on the floor where they'd had their picnic. It seemed so long ago, yet the thought of seeing him again energized her, and she was suddenly almost giddy. *Am I falling in love with him*, she asked herself. How was that possible when she still didn't really know the man? It must be infatuation, not love. You couldn't love a puzzle, could you?

On the ride down to Alexandria with Chris the next day, Kate told herself that repeatedly. But all the logic in the world didn't make a bit of difference. The moment she walked into the large rink where the South Atlantic Regional Competition was to be held, she scanned the milling crowd for a head of coffee-brown hair, a lean, muscular body, a pair of flashing blue eyes. Since the place was jammed with athletes, there were plenty of lean, muscular bodies. But none of them belonged to Sam.

It wasn't until she and Chris had completed the first of their compulsory gold-level dance patterns that she spotted her enigmatic lover. She had just left the ice and was crouching to put on her guards when her gaze collided with his. Holding a notebook loosely in his hands, he was sitting hunched over at the top of the stands. She was so startled that at first she didn't smile. Neither did he. There was, in fact, an odd expression on his face. But then she did grin and wave, and he waved back.

After the second compulsory dance Kate excused herself. Quickly she took off her skates, slipped into a coat and went out in search of Sam. He met her in the lobby with two steaming cups of coffee he'd just purchased from the snack bar.

"You look as if you could use this," he said, proffering a Styrofoam cup.

Kate accepted the hot coffee gratefully. "You're right. I could. Thanks."

He took her arm and led her toward one of the round Formica tables that was presently unoccupied. As he pulled a chair out for her and then walked around to the other side, she looked at him greedily. He was wearing his leather jacket again, but instead of jeans he had on gray flannel slacks that hugged his narrow hips. His hair had been cut recently, and the short crisp strands fit closely to the side of his head and around the back of his ears. His skin was slightly reddened from the cold out in the rink, as was hers, undoubtedly. She found herself imagining with startling clarity how it would feel to lay her cheek against the clean line of his jaw. It would be cool, faintly sandpapery. . .

"You're all done for a while now, aren't you?" he queried.

"Yes. The original set-pattern dance isn't until this evening. The free dance is late tomorrow afternoon." She was curious. "How did you know?"

Sam looked amused. "I studied the program. I've also been reading up on figure skating." He winked at her. "I now understand the physics of a swing roll."

"You did one with me."

"I did a lot of things with you that I didn't necessarily research beforehand."

When she blushed furiously, he reached out and squeezed her hand. "You're sweet. You're also good. I don't know that much about skating, but I watched all the couples you were up against. You and your brother stood out."

It was ridiculous how pleased she felt by his compliment. "I haven't seen the marks yet."

"I'll bet you're pretty close to the top." He took a sip of his steaming coffee and murmured, "So if that's where you want to be, that's where you're headed."

At a loss for an answer, Kate frowned. She didn't know where she wanted to be—except, maybe, in his arms.

When they finished their hot drinks and Sam went back out to cover the rest of the competition, she tried to find Chris. He wasn't hard to locate. As she rounded the corner where the standings had just been posted, he broke out from the throng of competitors and coaches milling there. Kate could tell right away that he had good news. He looked like a Boy Scout who'd just won every badge in the handbook.

"We came in third," he crowed. "And our gold dances are the weakest part of our performance. We're really rolling now, babe!" Jubilantly he snatched her off her feet and swung her around.

Kate did her best to match her brother's enthusiasm. But with Sam's disturbing remark still echoing in her ears, it didn't come quite as easily as it should have. What if they did win and had to continue practicing for the sectionals? Maybe that wouldn't be so bad, but what if they placed in the Easterns? Then there would be the nationals to contend with and heaven only knew what after that. The prospect gave her a chill that had nothing to do with the temperature inside the rink.

For the rest of the day Kate divided her attention between Sam and the practice sessions at a rink across town with her brother. During the novice pairs short program, she was able to spend an hour at Sam's side, explaining the moves and answering all his questions.

"What's that called?" he asked when the young pair on the ice went into a perilous maneuver that required the girl to arch back on one foot until her head touched the ice.

"It's a death spiral."

Sam frowned. "Aptly named. It looks to me as if she could get her neck broken doing that."

"Some of the pair moves can be dangerous," Kate agreed.

Sam turned toward her, the contrast between his sapphire eyes and his sooty lashes very sharp in the cold air. "How about dance? So far I haven't seen anything too bad, but you're only getting started, aren't you?"

"There are some tricky things in our program." Kate looked down at her mittened hands. Tricky was an understatement. Some of the maneuvers in their free dance were every bit as risky as that death spiral. She wondered what Sam would think when he saw them. Undeniably it gave her a little thrill to imagine that he might worry about her safety.

His gaze was intent and never left her face. "I don't want you to get hurt."

She tried to speak lightly. "Are you suggesting I hold back? That wouldn't be fair to Chris."

"I don't care about your brother. You're the one who's got me worried." He sighed and then grinned ruefully. "But I know damn well you're not going to hold back, and I'm not suggesting it. I've seen you in a competitive situation, remember? You're a thoroughbred. You'll give it everything you've got, even if you're telling the truth when you say you don't want the prize."

That evening as she and Chris waited to begin their performance in the original set-pattern dance, Kate ruminated about his statement. It was strange. She still didn't feel as if she really knew or understood Sam. Yet he seemed to comprehend her better than she did herself. He was right. Even if she wanted to fail, there was no way she could go out there in front of the judges and do anything but her best. An hour later, when that part of the dance competition was completed, she and Chris were in second place.

"What did I tell you?" he whooped when they'd read the standings. "Now all we have to do is knock 'em dead with our free dance tomorrow afternoon, and we're on our way!"

The rest of the evening and most of the next day were a blur. Kate was spending most of her time at the other rink, practicing. Except for occasional glimpses of Sam in the stands, she saw very little of him. She did, however, manage to snatch an hour with him in the afternoon. They had coffee in the lobby again and made a date to go out to dinner when her part in the competition was finished.

She was thinking of that when she slipped off her guards and stepped out on the ice for a warm-up. But once Chris took her hand and their names were called, her entire attention was focused on the music and the steps she and her brother had worked so hard to perfect. This dance was definitely the highlight of their program. Chris regarded it as his choreographic masterpiece, and he'd made it very plain that he desperately wanted it to come off right.

Under the pressures of a competition setting, that was asking a lot. Putting a blade down even a fraction of an inch wrong could ruin the performance. But there were no problems. They had practiced the four-minute routine with its complicated athletic footwork so frequently that Kate went through it like a robot, smiling at all the right times and never missing a beat.

To Sam and the other people in the stands, Kate and her brother's performance looked anything but robotic. With his fair good looks and her petite brunette beauty they made a handsome pair. But it was Kate that Sam watched. In her flame-red dress with her slim, perfect body she was youth and beauty. Gliding and twirling out there on the ice with what seemed like superhumanly graceful abandon, she was the embodiment of all that was desirable.

As his gaze followed her lithe movements, Sam felt a lump in his throat. He'd seen her skate before and knew she was good. But he'd never seen her quite like this. She was more, much more than merely good, and in a way it disturbed him. Talent like that deserved a showcase.

Some of the music was fast and acrobatic, and Sam caught his breath when he saw Chris maneuver his sister into moves that looked not merely dangerous but suicidal. It made him feel helpless and angry to see her taking such risks. Yet she never missed a step. She flowed as smoothly as the scarlet silk that covered her high breasts and clung to her subtly rounded hips.

It was the other part of the music, the slow, achingly romantic part that stirred Sam the most. There was no question that some of those graceful, sinuous moves were a poetic imitation of the act of love. To the couple on the ice it was merely an interpretation of the music, but to Sam it was an evocation. As Kate's brother held her waist and bent her back over his knee, Sam recalled how it had felt to hold her in his arms. The memory had been tormenting him for the past two weeks. As he studied the curving feminine line of her flexed body, his thinly banked desire began once more to burn.

When the dance was over and while the audience broke out in thunderous applause, Sam made his way out of the stands and down to where he'd seen Kate and her brother leave the ice. Looking pleased and excited, they were receiving congratulations from some of the other skaters and coaches waiting around for the posting of the standings. Sam hesitated until some of the crowd dispersed and then approached them.

"Congratulations. That was quite a show!" He kissed Kate lightly on the cheek and then turned toward Chris with his hand outstretched.

The last time they'd met, Chris had been patently suspicious of this new man in his sister's life, but he was now in too jubilant a mood to be anything but polite and friendly.

"Thanks," he said, taking Sam's hand and shaking it. "I think we have a chance."

"It looked to me as if you had more than a chance. In fact, I'll be surprised if you don't come in first."

Though Chris's eyes were alive with triumph and excitement, he quickly shook his fair head. "No, we didn't do well enough in the compulsory gold dance for that. But I believe we have a shot at second." He turned toward his sister. "What do you think?"

"I . . . I don't know," she stammered. "Maybe."

"Maybe, nothing!"

When the standings were posted, second was exactly where they placed.

"Hallelujah!" Chris shouted, turning to give Kate a hug. "We're going places, and that calls for a celebration. Let's go out on the town and buy ourselves a terrific dinner!"

Kate looked flustered. "Oh, but Sam and I . . . we'd sort of made a date," she mumbled apologetically.

Chris looked momentarily nonplussed. Then he grinned and shrugged. "Great. Marianne Summers is here. I'll ask her to be my date so we can make a foursome. How does that sound?"

It sounded terrible to Sam, but since Chris was Kate's little brother and she doted on him, there wasn't much he could say. He agreed good-naturedly.

An hour later they all met back in the lobby of the hotel where the competitors were staying. Since Sam was driving back and forth from Baltimore, he didn't have a room there. But he'd brought a tweed sport coat down with him and had exchanged his leather jacket for that.

Kate smiled when she saw him, thinking that even though the hotel was filled with long-limbed athletic males, they were boys whereas he was a man. He stood out like an antlered buck in a meadow full of half-grown yearlings.

She came forward and took his arm. "I'm sorry about our date. It's not like Chris to intrude that way, but this is a special occasion for him."

"For you, too." He smiled his understanding. "It's okay. It'll be fun. But I hope I can get you off to myself for a little while afterward. I've got to turn my story in tomorrow, and I need to ask you some questions."

As he spoke, his eyes glimmered appreciatively. They were sweeping over her with a look that was openly possessive. Kate felt herself grow warm all the way down to her toes. She had worn a clingy white angora dress and had made a special effort to look nice. The gratifying expression on Sam's face told her she'd succeeded.

A moment later they were joined by Chris and Marianne. The other young woman was a pretty redheaded skater whom Kate's brother had dated casually from time to time. As vivacious as a talk-show hostess, she was a nonstop chatterer, which meant there wasn't going to be any lag in the conversation.

They went to Benihana. It was a Japanese restaurant where dinner was ceremoniously chopped and cooked right at their table. The unconventional meal made an ideal background for a relaxed celebration. Yet there was some awkwardness. Kate couldn't quite put her finger on it, but she knew it was there.

For one thing, Chris kept referring to the "tough new practice schedule" they were going to need to adopt for the sectional competition coming up in six weeks.

Kate glanced nervously at Sam every time her brother made the reference. She couldn't help but recall Sam's ominous predictions when they'd had lunch at the Inner Harbor. Now they were coming true, and she had no idea what to do about it.

There was definitely something in the air. Though the two men who meant the most to Kate were scrupulously polite to each other, she sensed a subtle antagonism between them. From time to time she caught Chris looking suspiciously at Sam's strong profile.

The faint undercurrent of hostility wasn't entirely one-sided, either. Sam forced himself to be charming, but for some time now he had believed that Chris Coleman was selfishly refusing to recognize that his goals were not necessarily his sister's. As he sat across the table from the blond young man, he felt like walking around, seizing him by the scruff of the neck and giving him a good shake.

Dinner passed without incident, and everyone was perfectly civil, but both Kate and Sam were relieved when the other couple announced their intention to go dancing.

"How about you?" Sam inquired politely, turning toward Kate. "Would you like to go along?"

She shook her head. "I've had enough dancing for a while. Let's go back and work on your article."

"Okay." Sam's sapphire gaze shimmered. "That sounds like a great idea to me."

Chris cast his sister and her escort a suspicious glance, but Marianne was already leading him away from the table.

"I'll pay your half of the bill," Kate called out. "We can settle up later. Okay?"

"Okay," Chris said over his shoulder. Then Marianne whisked him out the door.

When the two were gone, Sam grinned at his date. "Don't worry about the bill. I'll handle it."

"Oh, but . . ."

He put out a hand to keep her from opening her purse. "My treat. It's worth a lot to have some time alone with you. It's been a while, hasn't it?"

Kate nodded and swallowed. What was going to happen tonight, she wondered. She did know that she wanted to be alone with Sam. She wouldn't admit it aloud, but she'd missed him desperately. All evening she'd kept looking at him, focusing on his hands, his broad shoulders, the details of his profile, just to assure herself that he was really there. Sometimes when she thought about their one night together, she felt as if she'd dreamed it. But the man next to her was no chimera. As he took her arm and helped her into her coat, he felt very real and solid. And very masculine.

Back at the hotel, he led her into the cocktail lounge. It was a quiet, dimly lit place and surprisingly empty. After they'd ordered, Sam leaned back into the booth and put his hands behind his head.

"You must be exhausted."

"No. I'm still high on adrenaline, I guess. What did you think of your first skating competition?"

"It was exciting."

Kate accepted her daiquiri from the waitress and then cocked her head at her escort. "As exciting as a football game?"

"It's sort of tough to compare the two. You don't generally see a herd of women in diamond chokers and mink coats wandering around at football games."

"True." Kate was amused. The outrageously ostentatious outfits worn by some well-heeled mothers of figure skaters—and sometimes by their coaches—were an in-joke. Occasionally a competition could seem as much a fashion show as an athletic contest.

"What's your article going to be about?" she asked.

"A general piece on the sport using this event as a particular example, I guess. I do have some questions I'd like to ask."

Kate was employing the bottom of her glass to make a design of wet rings on the cocktail napkin. "Okay, fire away."

Casually Sam pulled out a small notebook from his jacket pocket and began to flip through it. "First off," he said, "how are competitions scored?"

For the next half-hour Kate did her best to answer everything he asked. Apparently, he had been really doing his homework. Some of his queries were so technical that she wouldn't be able to answer them until she looked in the United States Figure Skating Association's fat rule book.

"Do you have that with you?" Sam wanted to know when she mentioned it.

"Well, not here. It's up in my room."

"Do you mind showing it to me?"

"Of course not, but—" she glanced at her watch "—it's getting awfully late."

He looked faintly amused. "I'll just walk up with you, and you can pass it to me under the door or over the transom. Whichever you prefer."

"Don't be silly." As he paid the bill, Kate stood and nervously smoothed her white wool skirt over her hips. She didn't know if she wanted Sam in her room or not. Part of her did, but on another level she was still afraid—afraid that she was in unknown territory and about to lose her bearings entirely. For someone who'd steered through life's twisting pathways as carefully as Kate had that was quite unnerving.

She'd never been a coward, though. As she rode up in the elevator, she was outwardly composed. So was Sam. But Kate wondered, as she glanced curiously at him from time to time, if his cool facade masked an inward excitement, and if it was anything like the feeling that was making her knees shake.

Apparently it was. For when she unlocked her door and stepped inside, he followed and pulled her against him before she'd even had a chance to turn on the light.

"I've been wanting to kiss you all night," he growled in her ear as he pushed the door closed with his body. Then his lips sought and found hers. Kate didn't try to pull away. But when he finally lifted his mouth, she hid her hot face against his shirt. It was unbuttoned at the collar, and she could feel the pulse in his throat against her forehead. It was beating as fast as her heart.

"Kate?" he questioned, laying his cheek against her temple and then moving his lips softly along her hairline.

"Do you want the rule book?" she mumbled into his throat.

"No." He laughed at himself. "That was just a not very clever excuse to get you alone. But I was getting desperate."

Her legs barely supporting her weight, she leaned into him, not pulling away but not lifting her face to his, either.

He ran his hand sensuously up her backbone and then tangled his fingers in her hair. A question hovered between them. "Do you want me to go?"

Her fists clenched against the nubby texture of his black V-neck sweater. "Sam, I'm just...I don't know...." She was painfully aware how incoherent she must sound, but she couldn't seem to gather her wits.

"What is it you don't know?" he asked probingly. "Me? Is that the problem?"

"I don't really... we haven't seen very much of each other." Even to her own ears she sounded pathetic.

He pulled her closer, cupping the base of her neck in his palm and rubbing his thumb gently in the sensitive hollow he found there. "Despite what happened between us before, you don't feel that you know me." As though her fingers and the tips of her breasts were delicate sensors, she could feel his baritone rumbling in his chest.

"Kate," he whispered, "two weeks ago when I said I wasn't sure what our lovemaking meant, I was lying."

Her heart seemed to come to a full stop, and though she wanted to ask a thousand questions, she couldn't say a word.

"I knew," he whispered. "I think I knew from the first what it meant. I just couldn't really trust it." He looked down at her quizzically. Her face was still hidden against his chest, and she seemed to be waiting.

"Maybe you don't know me," he continued after a moment. "But I know you."

"What do you know about me?"

Sam's mouth moved to the outer shell of her ear. "I know that you're a warm, beautiful woman," he murmured. "But anyone can see that. My radar has picked up more."

"What?" She finally stirred, tipping her face up to his.

Smiling down at her through the shadow, he touched his mouth to each corner of Kate's. "That you're cautious and particular, but that you can also be passionate and courageous," he replied.

"How can you tell all that?"

"From your skating, for one thing. But there are other ways. My God, woman, do you know how much I want you?" His hands moved down her back to the smooth curve of her bottom beneath the angora knit. She could already feel his hardness, and when he pulled her even closer the insistent demand of that aroused masculinity heightened the hollow ache she was beginning to feel between her thighs. Though her body was rapidly capitulating, some part of her still resisted.

"Enough to tell me pretty stories that aren't necessarily true?"

"No." His denial was rough but his hands on her body were silken. "I'm not lying in order to get you into bed. I'll prove it by telling you what other things I've learned about you," he rasped. "You're sensitive, honest and generous. All that is obvious from the way you're trying to help your brother." Still holding her hips firmly to his, Sam tipped her head back and kissed her closed eyelids and then the tip of her small, pointed chin. "You're a winner. You're careful, but when you give yourself to something your commitment is total. You hold nothing back."

Sam had reached up to slide the zipper at the back of Kate's dress downward. His other hand cupped her breast through the soft material, and his thumb began stroking a delicately provocative pattern around the stiffened nipple. "Don't you want me to tell you how I know that?" he questioned against the smooth skin of her throat.

Kate was hardly able to think at all, much less ask questions. All she could do was open her eyes in an unfocused stare that told him as much as any words were likely to. Bending, he scooped her up easily and walked across the room toward the bed. Kate was as pliant in his arms as a water reed.

"Because of the way you dance I know you don't hold back," he murmured against her lips. "And because I've made love to you."

Sam gently laid her on the bed. Then she felt his hands go to her feet and take off her shoes.

"I want to dance with you tonight, Kate," he said after he'd removed his own shoes and taken off his jacket. The mattress sagged as his weight joined hers. "But not on the ice or standing up on the floor. I want our dance to be here—like this. I want our bodies to move together in ways that only we will know."

As he pushed her dress farther down her shoulders and buried his head between her breasts, Kate twined her fingers in his hair. All her resistance had flown. There was a burning in her veins. She wanted the dance Sam had described as much as he and perhaps even more, because she was falling in love with him, although in many ways he was still a stranger.

When Sam lifted his head, she kissed him with all the ardor she possessed. And when he stripped the clothes from her and then from himself, she gazed up at him without shame or embarrassment.

"Trust me," he whispered as he came to her. "We're right for each other. We're building something very special. I know it even if you don't."

But she did realize it. She knew it in her bones and in her blood. Every cell of her body seemed to come to life at his touch, recognizing and desiring him. When his lean masculine body covered hers, making her feel as though she were surrounded by him, she knew that she had come home to a place she'd been seeking without even being aware of the quest.

Their coupling that night really was like a dance, she thought dazedly at moments. The touch of lips, the play of hands, the soft murmured groans, were a kind of music all their own: their lovemaking was a dance to an inner song that only they could hear.

Sam knew how to touch her so that she felt liquid and hollow with excitement. She touched him too, strok-

ing the velvet shaft of his desire so that he arched his
back and closed his eyes, his body taut with pleasure.

Greedily his lips found her breast, and something
deep within her quivered with delight at the rhythmic,
throbbing pleasure. Then he spread her willing legs
wide and thrust deep inside her, and a new pulsing
rhythm made her blood sing. She matched his movements with her own, a full partner in the splendid sen-
suality of their night dance. For both of them there was
a long, glorious moment when it ceased to be night,
when the darkness was incandescent and filled with
warmth. When that moment was over, they collapsed
into each other's arms, exhausted and utterly fulfilled.

8

THE NEXT MORNING Kate woke up earlier than usual. She was accustomed to sleeping alone. Finding her body nestled against that of a large, warm male was enough to make her eyes fly open as wide as they would go.

Sam had stayed the whole night. Now, as she lay on her side, he was curled tightly against her backside. They fit like snugly stacked spoons, and the realization made her think about what had happened between them. Scenes of their lovemaking flashed through her mind, and she felt warmth flood through her system. Her cheeks started to tingle, and she knew that she was blushing.

Half amused with herself but also half annoyed, she carefully dislodged her body from Sam's and turned gingerly so she could see him. He was fast asleep and didn't look as if he intended to wake up for hours. Kate glanced at her watch. It was only six-thirty, but she'd told Chris that she wanted to be back in Ellicott City to open her shop by ten o'clock. That meant he'd be showing up at her room around nine, expecting her to be ready to leave.

She frowned, struggling with the logistics of this. She supposed she could just dress quietly then go downstairs and get breakfast—leaving Sam to sleep until he felt like coming back to life. But that idea didn't appeal to her. Last night she felt they'd reached some sort of turning point in their relationship. This morning she wanted to talk to him. Just slipping away while he slept would be a letdown. Then she got an idea and smiled secretly to herself.

A moment later Kate got quietly out of bed and put on her bathrobe. Sam didn't stir. Keeping a careful eye on him, she picked up the telephone and carried it as far from the bedside table as the cord would allow. In a low voice she ordered breakfast for two.

She'd half expected that Sam might wake up when she started talking to room service, but he remained dead to the world. Replacing the phone, she stood for a moment looking down at the bed. Sam's arm was flung to one side, and the gold chain on his wrist sparkled in a weak ray of sun. The blanket and sheet had slipped down to his waist, and she was well aware that below it he was naked. Above the line of the sheet the morning light emphasized the muscular structure of his broad, smooth chest and shoulders. Against the white pillow his aggressive jaw and lean cheeks were shadowed with a new growth of beard. In contrast to all this blatant masculinity, his long black lashes lay like silky moth wings over the faint hollows under his eyes.

I'm in love with this man, Kate realized. The knowledge seemed to make her heart constrict, but it also brought a smile to her lips and a softness to her gaze. She'd never really been in love before; she'd been too cautious—preferring not to have anything at all rather than have something that wasn't exactly right. It was scary to realize that it had happened at last, but also exciting and fulfilling. Surely, after last night, there was a good chance that it would be right. Sam hadn't actually said he loved her, but his lovemaking had been so tender and so passionate that he must feel something for her. It was too early to speak of commitments. That would come, she told herself, when they'd been able to spend a little more time with each other.

Turning away from the bed on that thought, she picked up her purse, went to the door, opened it a crack and peered down the hall. At this early hour it was empty. Reassured, she left the door open and tiptoed outside. She'd noticed a beverage machine around the corner: now she made use of it. A few minutes later she returned to the room, carrying two Styrofoam cups of hot coffee. Kate had a theory about Sam, and now she was going to test it.

Setting one of the cups down on the bedside table, she perched on the edge of the mattress and slowly waved the other container under Sam's nose. On the second pass his nostrils quivered. Then his thick lashes opened, and his blue eyes struggled to focus on the cup moving like a slow, tantalizing pendulum in Kate's hand.

"Coffee," he croaked.

She smiled indulgently. "Yes, sleepyhead. Would you like some?"

His confused gaze lifted and then came to rest on the speaker. Kate's dark curls framed her pretty face in a deliciously dusky halo. Beneath her incredibly long lashes, her amber eyes were laughing at him. Wearing a cuddly pink bathrobe that matched the fresh color in her cheeks, she looked as bright and sweet as a newly scrubbed child. But she was not a child, he thought. His eyes dropped to the soft swell beneath the lapels of her robe, and he remembered the little inarticulate cries of pleasure she'd uttered as he'd made love to her. She was a passionate and responsive woman with a gorgeous, fine-tuned athlete's body—a body capable of kindling fires in him that he hadn't even known were there.

His blue eyes warmed. He pushed himself into a sitting position, accepted the cup she was proffering and took several sips from it. "Good morning, beautiful."

She blushed prettily. "I'm not beautiful."

"Right now you look like an angel who just dropped from heaven on an errand of mercy."

"What errand of mercy?"

"The coffee, of course." He raised the cup to his lips again, but all the while he drank from it, his eyes never left hers. She knew very well what was going on in his mind. He was thinking about last night. So was she. Underneath her robe she could feel her breasts tingling slightly from the caress of his gaze.

"I have only one criticism." He drained the cup and then set it down on the table at his side.

"What's that?"

"You're very pretty in that pink thing, but I prefer my angels in their birthday suits." As he spoke, he reached out and hauled her over on the bed next to him. Before she'd had a chance to catch her breath or issue a halfhearted protest, he was bending over her, his eyes flashing like impudent sapphires. "Now, let's see what's under all this terry cloth." His hands went to the ties of her robe, and he began undoing them. "As I recall, there are some very prime items. Ah, yes!" He pushed the lapels aside. "Eureka! Two gorgeous breasts!"

"Sam, stop it!" Kate protested between giggles. She batted at his marauding hands. "I ordered a room-service breakfast for us."

"I'd rather breakfast off you. Ummm, look at all these goodies!" He nuzzled the valley between her breasts, and at the same time ran an exploring hand down the curve of her hip to the flesh of her inner thighs. "You're the first woman I ever met with rock-hard thighs. It's really quite a fascinating sensation to have them wrapped around my waist."

"Sam!"

He lifted his dark head and grinned at her, his expression unashamedly wicked. "Let's try it again."

She pretended to pout. "It's not exactly a compliment to be told you have thighs like rocks."

"Isn't it?" He kissed her lingeringly and then whispered, "I love your hard thighs, and I loved being between them. In fact, I'm beginning to adore everything about you."

She caught her breath. His taut naked body now covered hers, and the feel of his warm hide against her skin was a tantalizing provocation. His words had done something to her insides. She felt herself quiver helplessly in his arms, and desire began to coil sinuously deep within her.

Sam moved his hands in a slow inventory: down from the sides of her breasts, along her narrow rib cage, to the indentation of her neat waist. While he softly kissed the underside of her jaw, his fingers traced the swell of her hip, finding at last the smooth plane below the jut of her hipbones.

There he curled his large hand, moving his thumb back and forth along the sensitive crease where her thighs joined her torso.

"Breakfast be damned, let me make love to you," he whispered huskily.

Kate's voice sounded breathless. "They could bring it at any moment."

"Room service is always late."

With a kiss that turned her bones to jelly, Sam silenced whatever protest Kate might have been ready to make. Helpless to resist him any longer, she wrapped her arms tightly around his shoulders and rubbed her smooth leg along the long muscular line of his hair-roughened one.

Growling with satisfaction, he lowered his head to her breasts and took a rosy crest between his lips. "I could get used to this, you know," he muttered.

"What?"

"Waking up with an angel in my bed."

His words excited her as much as the touch of his hands and lips. She arched toward him, offering herself without reservation, and in the next moments Sam accepted her gift in the same manner.

Fortunately, it turned out that he was right about room service. Their breakfasts did not arrive until twenty minutes later. By that time Kate was limp and sated, and she pulled the sheet up over her breasts, watching as he slipped into his slacks, then went to the door to get their meal. When he brought it back to the bed, the look in his dark blue eyes was eloquent.

"What I see is delectable," he growled, "and I don't mean the food. Though that's probably good, too," he added, his gaze finally dropping to the tray he carried.

Kate watched him put it down in the middle of the bed and then leaned over and picked up her robe from the floor. After she'd slid into it, she curled up against the headboard next to Sam.

"Just because I've got my slacks on, you don't have to wear anything," he pointed out, handing her a glass of freshly squeezed orange juice and then lifting a cover from a warm plate of crisp bacon and scrambled eggs.

Admiring the clean definition of his bare arms and shoulders, Kate picked up a sweet roll and began to nibble. "No," she said between bites, "but I think I would feel strange eating breakfast without clothes on."

He grinned at her. "Then maybe I should take my pants off again. I'd like to condition you to the idea of naked breakfasts."

Her gaze drifted appreciatively over his chest and flat belly. The gray flannel slacks partially concealed his hips and legs, but she knew by now they were all one could desire in a man. "You'll do the way you are," she murmured. When she looked up, she found that his eyes were a shade darker and sparkled with laughter as well as another emotion that seemed to make her heart swell. She felt buoyant with hope. Maybe she wasn't the only one falling in love. Fervently she prayed that it would be so.

The brief intuitive instant passed quickly, and Sam was once more the easygoing charmer who'd first bowled her over. As they ate their meal together, he teased her. Sometimes his jokes were outrageous, sometimes purely whimsical. But it didn't seem to matter what he said. Kate laughed at everything. She was happy—happier than she ever remembered being in her life. The intoxicating feeling bubbled through her veins like rare wine. It pleased her just to look at him and to know that right now, at this particular moment, he was thinking only of her. He was certainly the center of her world. She could eat breakfast in bed with him all day, she thought, savoring the closeness.

But the wonderful meal came to an end. Sam poured the last of the coffee from the pot, sharing it equally between her cup and his, and then set the tray down on the floor next to the bed.

"What are your plans for the day?" he asked. "I suppose you have to be getting back to your shop."

Kate nodded and then glanced at her watch. "Oh, my goodness, it's getting late. Chris will probably be coming up to get me around nine."

Sam looked at his own timepiece. "Well, then, I suppose I better be going. You probably don't want your brother stumbling in on us like this."

"No." Kate shook her head and then tried to explain. "It's not that I'm ashamed. I'm a big girl, and what I do is my own business. It's just that ·Chris is overprotective, and right now he's so fixated on our competing together that he gets upset if it looks like I'm being sidetracked."

"And I'm a sidetracker." Sam moved off the bed and stood up. "Since there's so little time, I'd better shower and shave."

Kate watched him stride toward the bathroom. Though he was still wearing his slacks, she could easily picture him the way he looked when she'd first seen him unclothed in the warming room. Only now that he was her lover she could appreciate his male beauty in an entirely different way than she had that first time. "Sam," she said softly.

He stopped and glanced back over his shoulder.

"You're not a sidetrack. As far as I'm concerned, you're the main line."

A slow, heart-stopping smile transformed his expression. "Same here." He crooked his finger. "Come on in and take a shower with me. It'll conserve time and water."

Matching his broad grin with one of her own, she scrambled off the bed and followed him, dropping her bathrobe as she walked.

Twenty minutes later Sam had pulled his pants back on and was tucking his shirt in while Kate, wearing jeans and a white turtleneck sweater, darted about the room stuffing the rest of her things into her suitcase. They'd spent more time in the shower than they should have. It was past nine, and Chris was bound to show up any minute.

"Now that you're going to be getting ready for the Easterns, I suppose it will be tougher than ever to see you," Sam grumbled as he shrugged into his tweed jacket.

"No, it won't. I've decided to hire extra help in the shop so I can have part of the weekend free."

Sam lifted an eyebrow. "Can you afford to do that?"

She couldn't, but she wasn't going to admit the fact. "It'll be okay. And it's just going to be for the next six weeks."

His expression lightened. "Well, that means we'll be able to spend some time together on Saturdays and Sundays. I'll call you about it tomorrow night after I've got this story written. Okay?"

"Okay." She abandoned her packing in order to put her arms around his neck and raise her lips to his. The offering was instantly accepted. When he kissed her, she melted against him and felt her knees go weak. *I'm in love*, she thought dizzily. *In love. I've waited a long time for this, but it was worth it. And it is going to be right—I'm sure of it.*

When Sam finally pulled away, he smiled down into her eyes for a long moment then shook his head ruefully. "I'd better leave."

She nodded and put her hand on the knob. Just then the door rattled with a brisk knock.

"Kate?"

It was her brother's voice on the other side. Sam's eyebrows swam upward, but Kate merely shrugged and turned the knob. She'd hoped to avoid this, but what did it matter? She wasn't ashamed that Sam was her lover, and Chris would find out sooner or later, anyhow.

He gaped when the door swung open, and Sam and Kate stood framed there.

"I was just leaving," Sam explained with a faint smile. Giving Kate's hand a final squeeze, he strode off. After he disappeared down the hall, Chris turned back toward Kate.

"That must have been quite a work session."

She was nonplussed for a moment and then remembered that last night she'd been going to help Sam write his article.

"He had a lot of questions to ask about figure skating," she agreed dryly and then turned back toward her packing. "I'll be ready in a jiffy. I just have to scoop up my toothbrush and lipstick." She didn't owe Chris any explanations, she told herself as she did a quick last-minute inspection of the room to see that nothing was left behind.

But her brother didn't ask any more questions or make any more sarcastic remarks. Indeed, he seemed almost unnaturally quiet. When she picked up her coat and suitcase and turned toward him, there was a worried expression in his eyes.

"How was your evening with Marianne?"

"Okay."

"Just okay? She's a very pretty girl."

"Yeah, well, she's also a very talkative girl. I've had better dates."

Kate gave him a look of mock exasperation. "The trouble with you, Christopher Coleman, is that you're spoiled. Because of those pretty golden curls you have on your head, women have been throwing themselves at you since you were a baby. It's time you learned to appreciate your good fortune."

But Chris didn't respond to her gentle teasing. "If you say so," he remarked brusquely.

A few minutes later she was settled in his red Corvette, watching his sharply etched profile as he pulled out of the parking lot and into traffic. All the way down to the car he'd been virtually silent, answering her questions in monosyllables. There was a crease between his eyebrows. Kate was beginning to wish that he'd say what was on his mind and get it over with.

Finally she couldn't stand it anymore. When they were out on the Washington beltway, she said crisply, "You've been awfully quiet. Is something bothering you?"

It was a full minute before he answered. "Maybe."

"Well, tell me what it is, for heaven's sake!"

Chris sighed. "I don't know if I should."

"This is driving me crazy. If you have something to say about Sam Ryder, say it and get it over with!"

Chris tapped the edge of the steering wheel. "He didn't just stop by your room to say goodbye this morning, did he? He spent the night."

"That's right." Kate folded her hands in her lap and stared straight ahead. "You might as well know that I'm in love with him."

There was a long pause, and then her brother sighed again. "I was afraid it was something like that. You wouldn't be acting like this otherwise. Have you told him how you feel?"

"No. But that doesn't change anything."

They rode along in an uncomfortable silence for several more minutes, then Chris cleared his throat. "Kate, there's something I have to tell you." He signaled to change lanes. When he'd successfully completed the maneuver, he rubbed one of his temples as if he were weary. It was an uncharacteristic gesture, and Kate wondered what was wrong. Chris was energy personified. He was almost never tired.

"I've been worried about you and this guy," he muttered. "I guess you know that."

"How could I not know? You've made it very plain. But I don't know what it is about Sam that's bugging you. You have no reason to be worried. Anyway, it's my business, not yours."

He shot her an irritated glance. "You're my sister, and I think that gives me some reasons. I know you've always been the one to look out for me. But this time I'm going to have to step in and take that role."

Kate blinked. "What in the world do you mean by that?"

"Okay. I suppose you're going to be furious about this, but I don't see how I can avoid telling you. I did some asking around about Sam Ryder."

"You what?" He was certainly right in guessing that she'd be furious. "You have no call to go prying into my private life!"

"I wasn't prying into yours," Chris defended himself. "I was prying into his. And, anyway," he added sulkily, "what I found out is common knowledge. All the media people know the story. The only reason you haven't heard it is because you don't travel in those circles."

Kate glared at him indignantly. "I can't believe this. You've been going around behind my back, gossiping about me?"

Chris made a disgusted noise in his throat. "What do you take me for? I never said a word about you. After I finally managed to drag Marianne away from that disco and take her back to her room, I had a drink with one of the other sportswriters at the competition. He was in the mood to drop a few tidbits about people he knew, and he happened to know a lot more about Sam Ryder than you do."

"I don't have to listen to this."

"No, you don't. I just thought you might like to get a little background on your Prince Charming."

Kate refused to dignify that with an answer, and for the next ten minutes a tight silence reigned in Chris's Corvette.

"All right!" she finally exploded after he'd exited onto Route 95. "Tell me what you found out."

He shot her another sideways glance and then, staring straight ahead through the windshield, began reciting facts.

"You know that gorgeous blonde, Carol Langford, the one who used to do the six o'clock news on Channel Ten, but who went to New York a few months back? Well, she and Ryder had the hottest affair going in town. They lived together for four years."

Silence stretched like a high-tension wire. Kate was unable to say anything. She felt stunned, as if she'd been knocked flat by a falling weight. Finally she managed to stammer, "But Carol Langford is . . . she's older . . ."

Chris completed the incoherent thought. "She's eight years older than Ryder, or at least that's what this reporter told me. He said Ryder was nuts about her, but the difference between their ages finally split them up." Chris gave her a look of compassion. "Kate, honey, you've got to know I wouldn't tell you this if I didn't care about you. I have to give it to you straight. A man doesn't get over a woman like Carol Langford in a hurry. My bet is that Ryder is just using you for a hot-water bottle while he nurses his wounds."

Kate's body felt anything but hot. A slow, numbing chill was creeping through her veins. She was utterly incapable of responding to Chris's statement. It was as if his words had turned her to stone.

Apparently guessing the reason for her sudden silence, her brother slanted her frequent sympathetic looks but said nothing more until he pulled up in front of her shop. Then he killed the engine and turned toward her. "Kate, I know you're upset. And I feel lousy for having to pass along this news. But what else could

I do? I couldn't just let you stumble around like a blind man in a minefield. I had to let you know the score."

Tentatively he put his hand out and touched her shoulder. But Kate didn't notice the conciliatory gesture. She nodded and carefully depressed the lock on the door so that it swung open.

"You look pretty rocky. Do you want me to come in with you? I could help you in the shop."

"No." The sound of her voice was strange to Kate. "I'll be okay. You go on."

"Are you sure? Honestly, Kate, I don't feel good about leaving you alone."

"Please. I'd rather be alone."

In the next few minutes she somehow managed to ward off all her brother's concerned offers of help. After he'd finally pulled away, she unlocked the door of Blithe Spirits and went in.

When she closed up shop that evening and climbed up to her apartment, the cash register showed that she'd made some sales, but she couldn't have guessed what they were. As she sat down at her kitchen table and stared numbly at the cold stove, she couldn't think what to do. Though she hadn't eaten since her breakfast in bed with Sam, she felt no hunger. Finally she opened a can of juice, drank it in several convulsive gulps and went to bed.

But almost as soon as she'd crawled between the sheets, she was dragged out again by the telephone. It was Chris calling to make sure she was all right. She assured him she was, brusquely cut off any further conversation and then stumbled back to bed. But once she was there, her eyes stayed wide open. All day she'd refused to think about what Chris had told her. Now her numbed mind edged a little closer toward the painful confrontation.

She'd known all along that there'd been other women in Sam's life. Everything pointed to it, even the way he made love. It wasn't Chris's confirmation of the fact that so distressed her. It was something else. Why hadn't Sam ever told her about Carol Langford? Why had he been so secretive? Kate groaned and shut her eyes tightly. Tomorrow she'd be able to figure it all out. Tonight she simply couldn't.

THE NEXT MORNING Kate woke up with leaden eyelids and a dull headache. She'd fallen into sleep like a victim overdosed on knockout drops. But she could no longer escape her problems that way. It was time to face the day.

Aching in every joint and feeling like a ninety-year-old misanthrope instead of her usually well-coordinated and chipper self, she stumbled into the kitchen. After glancing at the clock on the wall, she made herself a cup of coffee. When her fingers were curled around the hot mug, Kate stared for a long moment at the television set. Then, swallowing in the manner of a kid about to take a nasty dose of medicine, she walked across the kitchen and turned on the network news.

The first face to appear was Carol Langford's. Never taking her eyes of the newswoman's patrician features, Kate pulled up a chair and sat down in front of the set. It was an almost eerie sensation to watch the blonde on the screen. There had been so many things about Sam that Kate hadn't understood before. It was as if he were a scattered jigsaw. Chris had dropped this one missing piece into the center of it, and suddenly the puzzle had all snapped into place. This was the woman Sam had loved. Kate knew he must have loved her; he wouldn't have lived with her for four years otherwise. Chris's acquaintance had said that Sam was nuts about her.

And why not? Carol Langford was lovely. Not only did she possess an elegant, fragile beauty but also warmth, charm and intelligence. It wouldn't have mattered to Sam that she was so much older. Any fool could see that Carol Langford was a woman on whom the years sat well.

Her eyes still fixed on the screen, Kate tried to lift her coffee cup to her lips. But her hands were trembling so badly that she spilled the hot liquid on her bathrobe. For a long moment she stared down at the spreading stain. Then, jumping to her feet so abruptly that she knocked over her chair, she rushed to the sink. But when she rubbed cold water into the fabric, it only looked worse. Abandoning the effort, she switched off the TV and all but ran out to the living room. There she curled up on the couch and tried to calm herself by breathing deeply.

But when she opened her eyes, her gaze fell on the floor and she remembered their midnight picnic. How had it been when he'd made love to Carol Langford, she wondered. Images of the two of them in each other's arms suddenly burst in on her mind like Fourth of July rockets.

No wonder Sam had been such an expert in bed. He'd had plenty of practice with a woman who was not only beautiful and passionate but undoubtedly experienced. This new knowledge explained so many things: Sam's reaction that first morning when the TV had been on; the way his town house was decorated; his sensitivity over having to sell the place. Carol Langford had been the co-owner of that beautiful house, and he was still hurting because he'd lost her.

So where do I fit into this triangle, Kate asked herself dully. She could certainly see that Chris had been right about Carol Langford not being an easy woman to get over. Was he right about the rest of it?

Clasping her knees, Kate forced herself to face the situation squarely. Sam had never made a declaration of love. It could well be true that she was just a warm body for him, a way of passing the time. Kate drew her knees up even tighter against her chest and rested her forehead on them. Chris had referred to Sam as "Prince Charming." As far as she was concerned, that was no joke. All these years she'd been so careful, refraining from serious involvement to wait for the right man and the perfect love affair. In Sam she'd thought she'd finally found that. Now she had to face the fact that all of it might have been an illusion. He'd already had his big, dramatic, passionate love affair. Perhaps she was just the comic relief. Kate buried her face deeper in the folds of the terry-cloth robe covering her knees. Thank God it was Monday, and she didn't have to open her shop today. She felt too ill to do anything.

It was then that the phone started to ring. At first she tried to ignore its summons, but at last it penetrated her fog of misery, and she got off the couch and picked up the receiver. It was Sam.

"Hi, did I wake you? I was beginning to think you were unconscious."

"You didn't wake me."

"Good. I called early because I thought you might like to hear the article. I finished it late last night, and I have to turn it in first thing this morning."

For a moment her mind went blank. What article? Then she remembered the piece he'd been doing on the competition. "No, thank you. I'm sure it's very good."

"Not up to my peerless prose today, eh?" He sounded amused, but Kate felt no echoing response and waited silently. It was painful to hear his voice. She didn't feel up to talking to him or to anyone else.

"Well, you'll be able to read it in this evening's edition. Listen," he went on. "Since Monday is your day off, why don't we spend some time together? We could take in a matinee. There are several good movies in town."

"No, thank you, I don't think so." Kate looked down at her toes, focusing on them as though seeing them for the first time. "I have a lot of things to do today."

There was a brief pause. "That's too bad." He sounded disappointed. "Well, how about this weekend? You said you were going to hire extra help in your shop."

"Yes, but I haven't found anybody yet. I doubt that I'll be able to get away on Saturday or Sunday."

There was another silence, which she made no effort to fill. "Kate, is something wrong? You sound funny."

"Nothing's wrong. I'm just fine. Sam, I have to go now. There's something I need to do. Bye." Very carefully she hung up the phone. Then she went back to her bedroom, took off her stained bathrobe and climbed under the blankets. She would sleep for another hour, she decided, and then she would do that inventory she'd been trying to get to for the past month. The phone started ringing again. This time she pulled the covers up over her head and ignored it.

Later that afternoon Sam called her at the shop. That evening he telephoned again. Both times Kate had put him off with a vague excuse and ended her uncommunicative side of the conversation as soon as possible. She knew that she was not behaving reasonably. She should ask about Carol Langford and have this thing out. But she couldn't bring herself to do it—perhaps because she was afraid to hear what he might say. Every time the lovely blonde's name rose to her lips, she choked on it.

Monday night Kate resumed practice with her brother. She was silent and grim, and Chris, aware of what was bugging her, treated her like an accident case. Normally that would have been annoying. But she was too deeply immersed in her personal turmoil to care.

Tuesday night when she came home late from practice, Sam was waiting for her at the top of the stairs. She'd realized he was there when she pulled up to the curb and recognized his car. After sitting behind the wheel and staring at it for several minutes, she finally got out, hoisted her skate bag and trudged up the steps. The weather had turned bitterly cold, and there was a coating of frost on the handrail. She wondered why he hadn't stayed out of the wind in his automobile. It must be pretty unpleasant standing around up there on the landing.

Nevertheless, that's where he was. He had his fleece collar turned up and his hands in his pockets. Even in the dark she could tell that his eyes were slightly red from the cold. Despite everything her senses leapt at the sight of him. That fact was annoying, and when she spoke it was in an unnecessarily gruff voice.

"Aren't you afraid of getting frostbitten up here?"

"I was thinking about that, actually. I hope you're going to invite me in. I'm beginning to feel like an icicle."

"Sure."

Suddenly Kate was reminded of the time when he'd met her like this, and a bitter little shiver ran down her spine. Turning away, she put her key in the lock. Then she walked inside and flipped on a light. He followed and shut the door behind him. When she was inside, she let her bag fall to the floor. She knew she should offer him something hot to drink. But she didn't feel like offering him anything. Instead she sat down in a chair without bothering to take off her coat and folded her hands in her lap. "What can I do for you?"

He stood in the center of the room and regarded her quizzically. "What do you mean by that?"

"I mean, why are you here?"

The vertical line between Sam's dark eyebrows deepened. What was going on, he wondered. Three days ago Kate had been soft and cuddly and all that a man could desire in a lover. Now there was a force field around her that would zap anything within five feet, and though she wasn't saying much, her golden-brown eyes were snapping at him like an angry cat's.

"Kate, what's happened?" he asked baldly.

"Nothing."

He made an impatient gesture with his hand. "Come on, let's not play games. For the past couple of days you've been freezing me on the phone. Is it because your brother saw me in your room? I'm sorry about that. I should have gotten out of there earlier. But eventually he was bound to notice that we've become more than friends."

Kate took a deep breath. "It's nothing to do with Chris."

"What is it then?"

She shrugged. "Nothing much. I found out about Carol Langford, that's all."

As they stared at each other, Kate watched Sam's reaction closely. Idiotically she was half hoping that he'd merely laugh it off or look bored, or indicate in some way that the name was of little importance. But that didn't happen. Instead he turned noticeably paler, his body seemed to tense, and a wary look came into his eyes.

"What about Carol?"

Now who's playing games, Kate thought bitterly. "She's the person who owned that town house with you, isn't she?"

"Yes."

"And all those trips to New York—they were to see her."

"Only about business," Sam shot back defensively. "There were a lot of details to settle about the house."

Kate looked away wearily. "I can imagine."

Her tone galvanized him into action. He dragged up a chair and sat down so that they were directly confronting each other. "Who told you about Carol?"

"It doesn't matter."

He surveyed her tight expression. "Maybe it doesn't. All right, let's have this out here and now. Exactly what is it that's bothering you so?"

She turned her head back and met his gaze levelly. "Why didn't you tell me about her?"

"There wasn't any reason to."

"No reason?" Kate's delicate nostrils flared. "When we made love that first time, you asked me about my past. And I told you about Rod. Not that he made much of a story," she added dryly. "But I told you all of it. Why weren't you just as honest with me?"

Now it was Sam's gaze that slid away. "I guess I should have. But at the time it just didn't seem important."

"Not important?" Kate made a derisive noise in her throat. "A woman you'd lived with for four years?"

Sam grabbed her hand, and though she tried to drag it away, he held on tightly. "Try to understand. Carol and I split months ago. It was all over, and I didn't want to discuss it."

Kate stared at him fixedly. "You were really in love with her, weren't you?"

For a long time Sam was silent. Then he stood up, pushed back the wayward lock of hair that so often fell over his forehead and walked toward the window. Placing his large, sensitive hands on the frame, he looked out into the night. "Yes, I was," he admitted quietly.

9

KATE'S HANDS CLENCHED, and she squeezed her knees together. Sam's words continued to ring in her head, and she stared at his back until her eyes ached. He was still brooding at the window, looking out into the wintry night as if it held the answer to some riddle.

"What happened?" she finally heard herself ask. "Did you and Carol fall out of love?"

"Nothing as simple as that." He turned his head slightly so that she could see his profile. "It was the age thing. It just finally made it impossible for us to stay together."

"How do you mean?"

He rolled his shoulders. "When I first met Carol, I was twenty-six and she was thirty-four. Yet in a lot of ways we were at the same place in our lives. She was recovering from a divorce and starting to build her career. Baltimore was my first big-city job, so I was doing the same thing. We were both lonely, and we both needed someone. I thought she was a gorgeous lady and fell for her like a ton of bricks. At that time the gap between our ages didn't seem to make any difference."

"But later it did?" Kate was amazed at the calm manner in which she was asking these questions. From the tone of her voice Sam couldn't have known that his answers were like knife thrusts.

"Yes," he admitted slowly. "I wanted to get married, start a family. She wasn't interested in that kind of domesticity and considered herself too old for it. Then she got the offer from the network to move up to the big time in New York. I liked my job in Baltimore and didn't want to leave it. Yet I couldn't very well keep her from furthering her career." He turned to face Kate and took a step forward. "What I'm trying to say is that it wasn't so much a question of our falling out of love. For a brief time Carol and I were at the same place. Then our lives started moving in different directions, and there wasn't anything we could do about it."

"Does that mean you're still in love with her?" Kate asked.

Sam raked a hand through his thick hair. "There's no simple answer to that question. I'll always have feelings for Carol, but what we had together is over. When she left, I was pretty unhappy there for a while, but meeting you has made all the difference."

"I see." Kate felt as if she were looking through the wrong end of a telescope. Sam seemed a long way in the distance, and she gazed at him with almost scientific detachment. Maybe he believed what he'd just said, but she didn't. Carol Langford was only three hours away by train, and Sam obviously still cared for her. All of his behavior indicated that, and he'd even admitted as much. *So meeting me has made all the difference*, Kate thought cynically. How nice to be told that by offering the man her heart and her body without reservation, she'd unwittingly served as a psychological Band-Aid.

There was a bitter taste in Kate's mouth. "Sam, would you please go now? I'm tired."

"I don't think I've explained any of this very well."
He looked distressed, but Kate was too troubled by her
own feelings to try to analyze his. "I'm sorry I didn't tell
you earlier. I should have. I know that now."

"It doesn't matter." Kate's voice was expressionless,
but inside she was curling up and dying. "I'm very tired.
I don't really feel like talking anymore. Please leave,
Sam."

He gazed uncertainly at her as she sat ramrod straight
in her chair, a small, stony figure. "I hate to go like this.
We haven't really settled anything, and I'm not sure you
understand. It's not an easy thing to explain. May I call
you in the morning?"

"Sure." She hardly knew what she was saying. She
just wanted him to go away and leave her alone.

A few minutes later he did just that. When the door
had shut behind him and she'd heard the last of his
footsteps echoing on the stairway, she continued to sit
motionless in the chair. All the while she'd confronted
Sam, she'd been dry-eyed. Now tears began to leak
from between her closed lids and trickle down her
cheeks. Tomorrow perhaps she could be rational about
this. But for the moment she was at the mercy of her
chaotic emotions.

The next morning Kate didn't watch Carol Langford's television show. Nevertheless, the blonde's lovely
face was fixed permanently in her memory. Only when
she pictured her now, she didn't see her delivering the
news in her polished contralto. She saw her in Sam's
arms, pulling his head down to her breast and whis-
pering love words.

Kate buttered her toast with vicious little jabs. It hurt
to think about the two of them together. It hurt so much

that she didn't want to think about them at all. To that end, she dressed quickly and went downstairs, where she spent the morning frantically polishing everything in sight. Though it was bad for business, she left the phone off the hook. She didn't feel up to talking to Sam yet. *Maybe I'll be more sensible about this thing in another day*, she thought.

The following morning she tried. After fixing herself a mug of coffee, she turned on the television and sat down to watch Carol Langford again. She told herself she would look dispassionately at the woman Sam had loved and try to come to terms with the facts. But watching the beautiful newscaster was excruciating. Now that she knew about her relationship with Sam, Kate kept realizing things—how good they must have looked together, how perfect they seemed for each other. Against her will she found herself noticing small details such as the elegant line of the other woman's jaw, the humorous tilt of her well-shaped mouth, the way her honey-gold hair swept her brow. Sam must have studied all these things countless times and found them irresistible.

He'd implied that Carol's ambition had broken them up. But as Kate scrutinized the woman, she grudgingly acknowledged that Carol Langford didn't seem coldly ambitious. There was a warmth and generosity about her that projected even on television. She must have loved Sam very much, Kate mused. The age difference would have been far more awkward for her than for him. She must have been crazy about him. *Just the way I am.*

As Kate reviewed the things Sam had told her about his relationship with this woman, her hands tightened convulsively on her coffee cup. He had wanted to get married. That was when Carol decided to accept the job offer in New York. Sam believed Carol Langford had left him for that job, but what if it wasn't so simple? What if the blond newswoman still loved Sam and had ended their relationship only because she believed it was the best thing for him?

"She gave him up," Kate muttered with sudden intuitive conviction. "Because of the difference in their ages she decided that marriage wouldn't work, so she set him free."

Kate put her hand over her eyes and slowly massaged one temple with her thumb. She wanted to hate Carol Langford. She was burning with jealousy and hurt, and it would make it easier to bear if she could dislike the woman who'd captured Sam's heart. But it was impossible. She couldn't hate a woman who was both lovely and generous. And she couldn't blame Sam for loving her. She could only writhe with pain and disillusionment. In all honesty, she supposed it was really no one's fault that she'd blindly stumbled into the situation and gotten her own emotions shredded. Sam was a nice man; he hadn't meant to hurt her. He'd only needed comfort just when she'd been there to offer it. He should have warned her, but he hadn't—and now it was too late.

When Kate went downstairs to her shop, she felt even less able to talk with Sam than she had before. Yet she couldn't very well continue to leave the phone off the hook. Late that afternoon he got through to her.

"What's been going on? Have you been conducting a telephone marathon? I've been trying to call you since yesterday."

Kate took a deep breath. "Sam, don't call me again for a while."

"What?" He sounded stunned.

"I'm not myself. I'm upset, and I think it's better that we not see each other for a while."

"You can't mean that."

Kate rubbed the heel of her palm against her forehead. She was too distressed to choose her words carefully and blurted out her next statement in an unconsidered rush. "I do mean it. You never really cared for me. You were just using me to get over Carol Langford. Well, that's not what I'm looking for in a relationship."

"What? I can't believe you're saying this to me. You know it's not like that."

"I think it is like that. It can never be right between us again, Sam, because it was never right between us in the first place. I just don't want to see you."

She heard the door tinkle behind her as a customer came in. There was an explosion of temper on the other end of the line, but Kate only heard the first few words. Very carefully she replaced the receiver. Well, that was it, she told herself with a sick feeling. She'd probably never hear from Sam again. Already she wished she could recall her hasty words, but it was too late now. Pasting on a false smile, she turned toward the middle-aged woman who was fingering a silver tea service. "Is there anything I can do for you?"

FOR THE REMAINDER OF THE WEEK Kate worked like a dog in the shop and spent as few hours alone in her apartment as possible. It wasn't tough to do. Between her work and her practice schedule with Chris, she had almost no time to herself, anyway. What's more, Christmas was fast approaching, and there was shopping to be done. Saturday afternoon she used that as an excuse to avoid being alone and drove after work to the flashy new mall in Columbia. After picking up a light supper, she wandered around, looking at the displays and trying to decide what to buy for her brother and her aunt.

The trouble was that when she went browsing in men's wear departments, she kept seeing things that would look good on Sam. But that was because everything looked good on him, she thought, balefully eyeing a handsome pair of leather driving gloves.

She couldn't help wondering what she would have bought for him if their romance had still been on. Something ridiculously expensive, no doubt, she thought grimly. Something she couldn't afford. Maybe even a gold neck chain to match the one he wore around his wrist. Kate suddenly stopped cold in the middle of the aisle as something struck her. That gold bracelet was not the kind of thing Sam would have bought for himself. It was the sort of thing a woman gave a man. Carol Langford had given it to him. Obviously he treasured the bracelet since he wore it all the time.

Just then another shopper jostled her. Kate moved to one side to get out of the traffic. Pretending to admire a rack of ties, she rested her trembling hands on the glass counter. But she wasn't really seeing the ties, she was picturing Sam and Carol together exchanging gifts in front of a Christmas tree. In her mind's eye, it was a very romantic scene. Would he be buying Carol Langford a Christmas present this year?

Probably, Kate surmised with a little pang. Hadn't he said that he still had feelings for her? Maybe he would even go to New York and see her. After all, spending Christmas together must be a tradition with them by now. Given the special atmosphere that prevailed during the holidays—who knows—they might work things out, reconcile and live happily ever after.

Kate picked up a pair of gloves, grabbed a boxed set of socks and got in line at the cash register. She had to buy something for Chris. Wandering around the stores thinking about Sam wasn't doing her any good. She was going to stop it, she told herself fiercely. Tonight she was going to meet her brother at the rink, practice until she was ready to drop and not give Sam Ryder a thought.

In the days following the regional competition Kate had thrown herself into practice sessions with a will. Yet she wasn't skating well, and both she and Chris knew it. Her body seemed stiff and uncooperative. Her timing was off, and she kept missing steps that she'd performed easily before. Chris had been amazingly understanding. Despite his anxiety about the upcoming Easterns, he'd never criticized. And he never talked about Sam.

After her brother had told her about Carol Langford, she'd been angry for a while about his interference. But now she realized he'd only been trying to help her and that she should be grateful. Without Chris's revelation, who knew how long she would have wandered around in a dreamworld imagining that she was going to be the love of Sam Ryder's life, not knowing that the role had already been cast.

When Sunday rolled around, Kate thought seriously about calling off her evening session with Chris. Sunday was the night Sam's hockey team practiced. Kate didn't feel up to seeing him, and she didn't want to run into him at the rink, yet she couldn't quite bring herself to call Chris and cancel.

That night she arrived early to be sure that Sam's team would still be out on the ice. As soon as she walked in the door, she could hear the sound of clashing sticks. When she moved over to the Plexiglass window to look out over the ice, she spotted him immediately. He'd said he didn't have enough of a killer instinct to play good hockey, but it certainly didn't look that way. He was slamming the puck around as if he had a grudge against it.

It was funny, she thought, cocking her head as she watched him send the puck flying through the goalie's defense with vicious efficiency. Last time she'd stood here, she hadn't been able to pick him out. Now, despite the heavy disguise of his hockey gear, she recognized him right away. It was just because since then she'd seen him skate, she told herself. But Kate knew that wasn't the reason. She'd merely been very attracted before. Her feelings ran much deeper now, and that made all the difference.

But that had to stop, Kate told herself, turning away. You couldn't feel that way about a man who was hung up on someone else.

Kate changed her clothes in the ladies' room and then stayed there in order to give the hockey players plenty of time to collect their gear and leave. While she waited for their noise to die down, she leaned against the ledge that held the washbasins. Every now and then she inadvertently caught a glimpse of herself in the mirror opposite her. She was wearing a sweater, a sensible leotard and heavy knit leg warmers. No sexy little black dress tonight. As she remembered her own foolishness, she winced. How naive she'd been to imagine that she could win Sam by wearing a low-cut dress.

Glancing at her watch, she saw that it was five minutes after the hour. She couldn't hear any noise, so she pushed open the bathroom door and peered out. The lobby was deserted and all was silent. Quietly she padded over to the stairs and looked down into the warming room. It was empty. Reassured and yet also irrationally disappointed, she carried her bag down, settled on a bench and began to don her skates. Chris wasn't there yet, but ever since the night he'd blown a tire he'd been as punctual as a clock, so she was confident that he'd arrive soon.

Kate was just lacing up her left skate when she heard someone come in the door and walk down the stairs. It wasn't Chris. She could tell by the sound of the quick stride. She looked up, and her startled gaze collided with Sam's.

"I waited in the lobby for you," he said as he crossed the room toward her. "You didn't show up, so I went outside. But when I saw your car in the lot, I came back in. What were you doing—hiding?"

Since that really *was* what she'd been doing, Kate reddened slightly but didn't answer. Warily she watched as he hunkered down on the bench opposite her.

"What do you want?"

Sam looked derisive. "I want to talk to you, what do you think? Since you're so good at leaving your receiver off the hook, I've given up phoning."

"We have nothing to say."

"We have a lot to say. And this time I'm going to make sure it gets said." He eyed her levelly, thinking fast. He'd been going through hell all this week, and a part of him was furious about the absurd way she'd been acting. Another part of him, though, wanted to grab her and kiss her until she screamed for mercy.

Something about the manner Sam was looking at her mouth made Kate's eyes drop. Mutely she fingered one of the laces on her skate and waited to hear what he would say next.

"Kate, why are you treating me this way? I've apologized for not telling you about Carol. There's nothing more I can do."

"No, there isn't," she finally managed. "There's nothing you can do at all."

He raised his palms in a gesture of bewilderment. "Now what do you mean by that? Stop talking in riddles and be straight with me for a change."

She lifted her amber eyes, and Sam couldn't miss the resentment burning in them. "Like you were straight with me? You let me walk around in a fairy tale."

"A fairy tale?" His black eyebrows snapped together into a straight line. "Explain that, please."

"All right," she said in a clipped voice. "For a long time there I thought I was Cinderella and you were Prince Charming. Now I find out that I'm just an ugly stepsister."

"Ugly stepsister?" Abruptly Sam got up and stood with his back to her while he reined in his temper. Then he turned and raked her with a caustic look. "I can't believe that you could be so childish."

"Childish!" Kate started to stand up, but he pressed his hands on her shoulders and pushed her back down.

"Yes, childish! We've been lovers, we've known the most intimate moments, and now you're talking to me about Cinderella? Kate, I realize you're upset about Carol and that I should have told you. But I'm thirty years old, for God's sake. It would be strange if I hadn't cared about another woman by now."

"It's not just that."

"Then what is it?" he asked impatiently.

"It's not just a matter of your having cared for another woman. You lived with her for four years. Despite the difference in your ages, you would have married her if she'd been willing."

"But it's all over between us now. Why can't you understand that?"

Kate shook her head. "I don't believe it is, that's why. And even if I did, what you had with Carol Langford was a grand passion. Whatever it was we were having pales by comparison. I know now that if you want me it's only because you can't have her. That spoils it as far as I'm concerned—don't you see?"

Sam stared at her, his eyes like frosty blue stones. "Yes, I do see, as a matter of fact. I understand perfectly, and I'm not going to let you get away with it."

His tone was filled with such barely suppressed anger that Kate leaned away from him. "What do you mean by that?"

"I mean that by now I have a pretty good idea of what makes you tick. I've seen your fastidious little apartment, and I've seen you out on the ice. You're choosier than a judge at a Miss Universe pageant, and you're competitive as hell. All your life you've been a winner, isn't that true? Now you've got the idea that you're second best in my life, and you simply won't accept that."

Kate's temper slipped, and she glared at him. "I am second best! How could I be anything else?"

"Oh, grow up!" Sam snorted. "You're a romantic. But this isn't a fairy tale, Kate. This is real life, and relationships with people in real life are more complicated than the brothers Grimm knew." He leaned forward, hunkered down, grasped her shoulders and forced her to meet his penetrating gaze. "You're in love with me," he grated. "Oh, yes, you are, don't try and deny it. You wouldn't have slept with me otherwise. I knew it from the first, and it scared me because I'd just been through hell with Carol and I wasn't sure I was ready to chance it again. But I'm not scared of that anymore, and I'm not backing off. I know I want you and that we're right for each other. Yet you're ready to throw away what we could have because it doesn't live up to your romantic standards. How the hell do you think that makes me feel?"

Kate was shaken by his intensity and too upset to be really sure of what he was saying. "You have no right to talk to me like this!"

"We're lovers. We both know it's not a casual thing between us. If I don't have the right, then who does? And while I'm at it," he continued relentlessly, "there's something else I want to say. Carol and I broke up partly because of her ambition. She wanted a big-time career, and I wanted a wife." Sam's hands were still curled around Kate's shoulders. Now they tightened. "What do you want?"

Kate's cheeks were pale, her golden-brown eyes huge in her heart-shaped face. "I don't understand."

"Don't you? Ever since we met you've been reading to me from one script and acting out another. You say you aren't ambitious for a skating career and that you want to be with me. Yet because of this thing with your brother, you've made it practically impossible for us to be anything but ships passing in the night."

"I explained that was only temporary," she protested.

"Is it really, though?" There was a white line around his mouth, and a muscle in his jaw ticked. "You accuse me of not being honest with you. Have you told me what I need to know? You're good out there on the ice, and you could probably get to the top if you wanted. I didn't stand in Carol's way when she decided to grab the brass ring. And I wouldn't try to stand in yours, either. But before it gets any thicker between the two of us, you need to be straight with me."

"I've always been straight with you. You're the one who's been keeping secrets," Kate shot back huskily.

Sam surged to his feet. "I think you're confused, Kate, and that you have to make some decisions."

She stared up at him and suddenly noticed that he looked very tired. He was pale, and there were blue shadows under his eyes. For a moment she could almost believe that he was afraid of getting hurt again—only this time by her. Despite her confusion and resentment, she felt the impulse to reach out toward him. Then he put his hands on his hips, and her eyes dropped to his wrist. As if it were a warning signal, the gold chain he habitually wore glinted dully in the muted light.

Kate turned her face away. She couldn't say anything to him. Somehow he'd switched everything around and made it sound as if this were all her fault. His relationship with Carol Langford was the issue, not her skating.

"Not talking, eh?" he finally remarked. "All right, I'll go then and let you think it over. If you come to any conclusions, let me know, will you?"

He turned and stalked away without another word, and Kate was left in the empty warming room staring after him, a hollow feeling in her chest. A moment later she heard the swinging doors slam as he pushed past them.

She had been so engrossed in her confrontation with Sam that she hadn't even given Chris a thought. She was startled when she heard footsteps on the stairs again, and her slim blond brother rounded the corner.

"Are you okay?" he asked.

"What do you mean?"

Slowly Chris began walking toward her. "That was quite a little scene you just had with Ryder."

"Were you listening in on it?"

"I was up in the lobby, and from what I could hear it sounded as if I'd better stay there until you two had it out." Chris looked apologetic. "I would've come down if there'd been any trouble."

"What do you mean? Sam isn't a violent person."

Her brother's brown eyes were troubled. "I don't know. He sounded pretty angry." There was a pause. "That crack he made about your skating . . . He wasn't telling the truth, was he? You want to win the Easterns as much as I do, don't you?"

Kate stared up at her brother and was unable to think of a thing to say. There was a strained cast to his mouth that made him look almost as upset as she felt. Bending over her boot so that he couldn't see the expression on her face, she began to tighten the laces. Because her fingers were stiff and uncoordinated, it was all but impossible, and she finally went ahead and tied the skate even though she knew it was too loose around the ankle.

"You haven't answered my question," Chris demanded.

Kate put her palms on her knees and looked up at him again. "You knew when we started that I wasn't as enthusiastic about the idea as you."

"Are you telling me that Ryder is right, that you really don't want to go on with what we're doing?"

"I'm not backing out on you, Chris."

"That isn't the question I asked."

Glancing down at her skate, Kate swallowed. It was a custom-made boot that gripped her foot tightly, so it really wouldn't make a lot of difference if it wasn't laced properly, she told herself.

"Kate?"

At last she looked up. "Please, I'm upset, and I just don't want to talk about it now."

Chris's brow began to wrinkle. But finally he shrugged. "Okay, I guess I can understand that. Are you too upset to practice?"

She was, but she didn't have the heart to say so. "As long as I'm here, we might as well get some work done."

"Are you sure?"

"Why not?"

Chris slumped down on the bench beside her. "Why do I get the feeling that you're going to an execution instead of a practice session? This is supposed to be fun, Kate."

"Usually it is. I'm just not in a fun mood right now. But that doesn't mean I can't work. We've paid for this ice time. Let's stop talking and get out there."

Sighing, Chris began to unzip his bag. After he'd put on his skates, Kate pushed herself off the bench and walked out onto the ice with her brother following close behind.

"You'd better do a good warm-up," he advised. "You're so uptight you're walking stiff-legged."

"Okay." She didn't need to be told that she was uptight. Every muscle in her body felt knotted. Her shoulders ached from tension, and the rink seemed unusually frigid, the cold cutting to the bone. Even though she worked for ten minutes trying to get loose, she never did really warm up. When she gave up and skated over to Chris, her body still felt tense.

"Do you want to work on the gold dances for a while?" he asked. "That's where we're weakest."

Kate leaned against the boards and slid her blades back and forth on the ice. "All right. Let's try the Argentine."

Chris started the tape, and for the next fifteen minutes they labored through the tango. It was a set-pattern dance skated to Latin American music and required strong, fast edges and considerable élan. Though there were some rapid steps and turns, other movements needed to be executed with prolonged free leg extension, flowing movements and in perfect unison.

The latter seemed to escape them entirely. They were so far off that several times they had to stop before a pattern was even completed and start again. Kate knew it was her fault. Despite her efforts to think only about the dance, snatches of the argument with Sam kept popping into her head. He'd made some pretty devastating charges. She wanted to ignore them, but they kept running through her mind.

At the next pause in the music Chris stopped so abruptly that she almost slammed into him. "This just isn't working. I don't feel like doing a tango, and obviously neither do you."

Kate sighed. "I'm sorry. I know I messed up the twizzle," she said, referring to a complicated turn.

"It's more my fault than yours. I never did like the dance, anyhow. I always feel like I'm doing a poor imitation of Rudolph Valentino."

She gave a self-conscious laugh. "I know what you mean. Maybe it would help if we both carried roses in our teeth."

Chris smiled at the feeble joke, but she knew that he wasn't particularly amused.

"Do you want to run through the free dance?" she asked.

"Well, I suppose we can give it a try."

While he went to change the tape, Kate stood in the middle of the ice, thinking once more about Sam. She wasn't exactly proud of her behavior these past few days. Perhaps it hadn't been logical or adult to hide from him, but she couldn't help her feelings. Confused and hurt, she was going with her instincts to protect herself until some of the rawness healed over and she was better able to cope with the situation. That made her think again of what Sam had said. "You've got the idea that you're second best in my life, and you simply won't accept that."

He was right, Kate realized. That was exactly how she felt. She loved him, but it hurt her pride to think of herself as his second choice. She wanted to be first. But it wasn't quite the fixation that he'd made it sound. She knew perfectly well that she couldn't always come out on top, and though she was competitive, she'd learned to take defeat gracefully when she had to. There was no way she could have gone as far as she had in figure skating without getting a lesson or two in humility.

But athletic contests could be put in perspective, while the emotion she felt toward Sam couldn't. Love was too important to settle for second best, she told herself on an anguished inner cry. There she did need to be a winner. And if she couldn't be first with Sam, then perhaps it was better to be nothing at all.

"Let's run through the whole thing and see if we can get a little more expression in the slow part," Chris suggested as he skated back out toward her.

"Anything you say."

He cocked his head. "You don't look too great. Are you sure you're up to this?"

"No." Kate offered him a weak grin. "But then I've been through this number so many times that I ought to be able to do it in my sleep."

That wasn't quite true. There was no way to do this complicated routine without concentrating entirely on it. But Kate's intentions were good. She didn't want to think about Sam anymore. She wanted to lose herself in something that would banish him from her mind.

At first it seemed to work. By sheer effort of will she dragged her thoughts from the scene in the warming room and focused on the erect carriage and smooth knee and body movements that were so important in the early section of the dance. But halfway through her concentration wavered, and she was thinking once more about Sam.

The things he'd said about her skating had come as a surprise. She'd known that he believed Carol Langford had walked out on him for a fancy job in New York. Now he was practically accusing her of doing the same thing. But it was completely untrue, Kate thought. Skating was far less important to her than her personal life. She'd give skating up in a minute if she thought she could have the kind of relationship with Sam that she wanted.

But that notion led to an even more disturbing one. When Sam made that remark about Carol Langford's career, she should have told him that he might be all wrong. She should have told him that she suspected Carol had left him out of noble self-sacrifice rather than coldhearted ambition. Why hadn't she?

But Kate knew the answer to that. She hadn't mentioned it because she didn't want Sam to know. If he was aware of Carol's altruistic motives, he might go to see her and demand a reconciliation. Shame flooded through Kate. It had been selfish and despicable of her to withhold that information. Though it was just an intuition, in her heart she felt almost certain that Carol Langford had left Sam out of purely selfless motives. *I should have told him*, she thought.

At that moment Kate realized that Chris was about to put her into the lateral twist. She'd been so preoc-

cupied that she'd been skating like an automaton. But
for the twist one couldn't be a robot. She needed to be
all there.

She hesitated, trying to tell Chris that she couldn't do
it. But it was too late. His hand was already around her
waist, and there was no way for either of them to back
out. But it was also too late for Kate to retrieve her timing. The next second was a blur of mismatched hands
and falling bodies. There was an excruciating crunch,
and Kate found herself sprawled facedown on the ice.

Chris had tumbled over on top of her. But he was up
in a flash. "Kate, Kate, are you all right?"

For a long moment there was no answer. Over the
years she'd taken hundreds of falls. Some had been
quite painful, yet most of them she'd been able to walk
away from. This one was going to be different. For a
second she was, in fact, unconscious. When Chris's
voice got through to her, Kate began groggily struggling to get up, but her right leg felt as if it wasn't there.
She sank back down on the ice, her face ashen and her
limbs trembling.

"Are you all right?" Chris asked again.

"No," she finally told him. "I don't think I am all
right. I think you're going to have to carry me out of
here."

He did just that, putting his arm under her shoulder
and bearing most of her weight while she stumbled off
the ice. When he'd gotten her out into the warming
room, he sat her down on a bench under a light and
gazed intently into her eyes.

"Why are you staring at me?" Kate mumbled.

"I'm checking for a concussion. You ought to know
that."

Normally she would have known, but right now her brain didn't seem to be functioning properly. She watched numbly as he moved an index finger back and forth in front of her face.

"You seem okay," he said at length. "Why don't you rest a bit."

She did as he advised, but things didn't improve. For a long time she lay on the bench with her hands over her face while her brother looked down at her anxiously. Since the South Atlantics everything had been going steadily wrong. Now this!

She started to tremble uncontrollably, and her teeth were chattering. When the pain started, she spread her fingers and met his eyes.

"Chris, I think we'd better find an emergency room. There's something badly wrong with my knee."

10

"IS THERE ANYTHING ELSE I can get you?" Chris was hovering in front of the couch where Kate lay with a blanket over her legs. The crutches she'd been hobbling around on for the past couple of days were propped against the chair next to it.

"No, I'm all set. It's just a matter of negotiating the stairs." She managed a smile. "If you're willing to carry me down to the shop when I feel up to it, I can take care of the rest by myself."

Chris shifted from one foot to the next, and his brown eyes were troubled. "God, Kate, I'm so sorry. This is all my fault."

She stared at him in surprise. It had never once occurred to her that the accident was her brother's fault. Quite the contrary, she knew it was hers because she hadn't been concentrating. In fact, ever since coming out of the arthroscopic surgery that the doctor recommended when Chris had whisked her to the emergency room, she'd been feeling guilty because his hopes for placing in the Easterns were now ruined.

But when she told him that, he only shook his head. "No, this is my doing," he insisted, gesturing at her bandaged knee. "I knew you were in no shape to be out there working on our routine." He looked down at his feet. "The truth is that I was in no shape to be out there, either. I was pretty upset about what I overheard Ryder say."

Kate tilted her head. "What do you mean?" Aside from the few words they had exchanged in the warming room that evening, they hadn't really discussed the argument with Sam that Chris had overheard.

Chris dropped into the chair opposite the couch and rested his elbows on his knees. For several seconds he gazed earnestly at his sister.

"Kate," he finally said, "I think I always knew that you weren't as gung ho on the competition bit as I was. But I wanted it so much that I just ignored the facts. And now that I've finally admitted that to myself, I feel sick about what I've done. You've got your own life to live, and you don't need me messing it up for you."

"It's not your fault," she put in quickly. "I agreed to do it."

"You agreed because I pressured you." He put both hands up to his temples and ran his slim fingers through his fair curls. "When I overheard what Ryder said to you about it, I knew in my heart he was right. With the Easterns so close, I didn't want to face up to the fact. But my conscience was bothering me when we were out there on the ice. I kept thinking about the situation, and that's why my timing was off."

"My timing was off, too."

Chris laughed ironically. "Was it? I suppose so, but I was too busy worrying about myself to pay much attention to your problems. Which is the way it's been with us too much of the time," he added. "Hasn't it?"

"Believe me, I was preoccupied, too," Kate insisted.

He laughed shortly. "We were a great pair."

"We *were* a great pair." She held out her hand, and Chris immediately got off the chair, knelt beside her and took it.

"You're right," he agreed. "We had something special. But a lot of that is you, Kate. You have something special, both on the ice and off." He grinned ruefully. "But now I'm going to have to find myself another partner, aren't I?"

Slowly she nodded. "'Fraid so. Do you think you can?"

"Yes." Chris gave her the boyish lopsided smile that had been dear to her ever since she could remember. "You know how I am—I've already started putting out some feelers." He got up and resumed his seat opposite the couch. "The Wilmington club has several girls looking for partners. I'm driving up there this weekend to check two or three of them out."

Kate's eyebrows began to elevate. "You're not letting any grass grow under your feet."

"You don't mind, do you?" He sobered. "Maybe it seems a little callous, but you're out for at least a month, and we agreed that you didn't care to come back next year." Chris glanced down at his feet and then up at her. "Since I broke up with Elise, I've been doing a lot of thinking. Computers just aren't enough for me and neither is marriage. She was right about that, I have some growing up to do. But one thing I do know. What I want right now is a career in skating. I want to perform in front of audiences. And now, thanks to your help, I honestly believe I have a shot at it." Chris's brown eyes were earnest.

"You do!" Kate quickly reassured him. "You're good and you want it—so go for it!"

Leaning forward, he squeezed her hand again. "You're a great sister, you know that? Whenever I've needed you, you've been there. Not only are you pretty and talented, you're just plain nice. I'm a lucky guy!"

Kate laughed at him. "Well, I'm glad you finally noticed."

"I've been noticing a lot of stuff lately." Chris stood up and began to pace restlessly around the room. "There's something else I want to say to you." Over his shoulder he shot her a worried glance. "Out there on the ice I wasn't just bothered about the skating thing. I was also feeling bad because I was beginning to realize that I'd been wrong about Ryder."

Kate was immediately on the alert. "What do you mean?"

"I mean that I have to respect the guy, and I've changed my mind about him. He wouldn't have talked to you that way if he didn't care about you." Chris turned and faced her squarely. "I think I gave you a bum steer. I think Ryder might be as hung up on you as you are on him."

"Then he must need a harem," she snapped, "because he's already hung up, as you say, on Carol Langford."

"I don't know about that." Chris shrugged. "It didn't sound that way in the warming room. All I'm saying is that maybe you better talk to him again and give him a chance. If you really like him, that is."

Kate was silent, and Chris studied her for a moment sympathetically. "I can see that you don't want to talk about it now."

"No, I don't."

"Okay, I'm easy. You don't have to tell me anything you don't want to. As soon as you want me to take you down to the shop, give me a call. Are you going to be okay until then?"

"I'll be fine," she assured him, managing a smile.

Chris took her at her word, and a few minutes later he left her alone with her thoughts. Mindful of her knee, she shifted carefully on the couch. So much had happened in the past two days that she'd had very little time to think. Fortunately, arthroscopic surgery, a relatively new therapeutic procedure, required very little recovery time. Her doctor had been able to remove the torn cartilage in her knee by using a miniaturized television camera and tiny instruments. The required incisions were so small that they could be covered with a Band-Aid. Consequently Kate had been able to leave the hospital late the next afternoon. Although the surgery itself was surprisingly easy, it did mean that her life was changed. After a few weeks of physical therapy, she could go back to skating. But she knew she'd never again want to be a competitor.

Part of her was relieved that the Easterns were out of the question this year. But she was also a little disappointed. She and Chris had been good, and on some level she'd been looking forward to showing the skating world that she could still do it. Maybe Sam had been right. Maybe beneath all the grumbling she'd done, she really had wanted the thrill of winning another major competition again. But she'd never wanted it enough to walk away from him. Now it looked as if she'd lost everything.

Restlessly she readjusted her position. As she lay in her hospital bed after surgery, Sam's image had been in her mind. She still loved him—that hadn't changed. Several times she almost called him from the hospital to ask him to come to see her. But what would they have said to each other?

In a way, they'd said it all in the warming room. Sam cared for another woman whom he couldn't have, and Kate was supposed to be adult enough to accept that. Somehow she couldn't bring herself to do it.

Kate put her face in her hands. She wanted to see Sam again. She wanted to talk to him, to hear his voice. Suddenly she felt very lonely. Her apartment had always seemed like a sanctuary before. Now wherever she looked it was full of reminders of the man she loved.

"I was stupid," she muttered aloud into her fingers. "It doesn't matter that I'm not first with him. It only matters that I have him, even if it's only for a little while."

Kate lifted her head, a resolute expression on her face. Tomorrow she would call Sam.

But the next day when she got up the courage to dial him at home, he wasn't there. After some reflection and another fortifying cup of coffee, she called the *Globe*. Through the switchboard operator she asked for him by name, but the man who answered the phone was not Sam.

"Barrows here, what can I do for you?" a gravelly masculine voice inquired.

"I'm trying to get in touch with a Mr. Sam Ryder."

"Who's calling?" He sounded impatient, and in the background Kate could hear contentious voices, the muted clack of word processors and the sound of scraping chairs and scurrying feet.

"My name is Kate Coleman. Could I talk to Sam, please?"

There was a long pause, and then she heard the man named Barrows shout a question about Ryder's whereabouts. A second later he returned to the phone. "Sorry, he's out of town."

"Oh?" Kate was suddenly apprehensive. "Can you tell me where he's gone? It's important."

"New York, isn't it?" she heard him ask someone nearby. "Yes, that's right." Once more the disembodied voice returned to the line. "He's gone to New York, but he's expected back in a couple of days. Can I leave a message?"

Kate's hands were clenching the receiver so tightly that they were beginning to feel numb. "No," she said very softly. "No, that's all right." Then she hung up and sat staring blankly off into space. So he was in New York. She knew what that meant. He'd gone to see Carol.

The rest of that evening and the following day passed by without Kate really paying much attention. After the call to the *Globe*, a gray fog had descended over her spirit. She slept most of the time, hobbling to the kitchen and the bathroom on her crutches only when necessary. Chris called every now and then to ask if she wanted his help. The second day she took him up on the offer.

"Can you carry me down to the shop? I need to get out of the apartment, and I think once I'm downstairs I can manage well enough to stay open all afternoon."

"Are you sure?" he queried. "There's no place to lie down."

"There's a comfortable chair, and I can put my feet up on a stool. All you have to do is bring me down. I can make it back up on my crutches. I'm getting to be pretty good on them."

Though Chris was doubtful, he agreed to do what she asked, and Kate was intensely grateful. The walls upstairs were beginning to close in on her. What was Sam doing now, she kept asking herself. Had he and Carol Langford ironed out their differences? Were they lovers once more? Having such thoughts was like probing a fresh wound, but she couldn't seem to help herself.

The day in the shop was long and uneventful. Even though the Christmas buying season was now in full swing, the weather was overcast, and she only had a few customers. It was so quiet that she had plenty of time to read a paperback that she'd been meaning to get to. But the words only blurred on the page.

Finally she shut the book with a snap. The problems encountered by its hero and heroine seemed far less compelling than her own. Once again she found herself thinking about Sam. Was he still in New York? Or had he come back? And if he was once again in Baltimore, was he alone?

With an abrupt twist of her wrist, Kate tossed the book on the floor. It landed on the rug with its pages splayed open, and she stared at it grimly. She had to stop thinking about him, she told herself. If she was going to get her life back on track, she'd have to exercise a little self-control, which was something she certainly hadn't managed to do whenever he was around.

As she contemplated this fact, there was a bleak look in her golden-brown eyes, and she wondered if she would ever again in her life lose control the way she had with Sam. Would she ever again know the joy he'd brought her? Just then two of the several antique clocks mounted on the wall began to chime the hour. Kate glanced at her own watch. It was five o'clock, time to close the shop and go upstairs.

She had assured her brother that she was capable of getting back to her apartment. But twenty minutes later when she was outside on her crutches and facing the steep wooden staircase that led up to the second floor, she didn't feel so confident. The maneuver was going to be as tricky as anything she could do on the ice. *But I'm a world-class athlete*, she reminded herself dryly. Putting her crutches up on the first step and holding on to the railing with one hand, she hoisted herself.

Kate was a third of the way up the staircase and panting with exhaustion when she heard a male voice exclaim, "What on earth are you doing?"

Swiveling her head, she looked over her shoulder and saw Sam standing at the foot of the steps, his long legs planted wide apart, his hands on his hips. He stared at the crutches and then focused sharply on her pale face.

"What have you done to yourself?"

Kate said nothing, but all at once she felt her lip tremble and had a wild impulse to collapse on the steps and burst into tears. As she struggled with that, she realized Sam was taking the stairs two at a time. In the next instant he had snatched the crutches from her hands, laid them down and scooped her up into his arms.

"You were headed for your apartment, weren't you?"

"Yes," she managed through chattering teeth.

His arms felt like oak as he carried her the rest of the way, but she was too tense to relax in them. She avoided looking into his face, concentrating instead on the zipper of his jacket.

"Have you got your key?" he demanded when they reached the landing.

"The door isn't locked."

Sam shot her an outraged look. "Oh, great! What would you do if there was some thug in there waiting for you? Hit him with your crutch?"

Kate maintained a mutinous silence. Normally she kept her door locked. But when Chris had taken her downstairs this morning, she just hadn't thought about it. And what right did Sam have to criticize her? It was none of his business!

Without saying anything more on the subject, he pushed open the door, carried her inside and carefully laid her down on the couch. "I'll be back in a minute."

When he strode from the room, she began to struggle with her coat and managed at last to take it off and toss it over the back of the sofa. She'd worn a fluffy pink top and a full burgundy wool skirt. Despite everything she congratulated herself that even though she didn't have much makeup on and probably looked like death, the color of her sweater at least was becoming. Of course, it was absurd to be thinking in such terms, but her mind was racing in all directions, trying to cope with a hundred different questions, none of them very logical.

A moment later the door swung open and Sam, holding her crutches, stood on the threshold, his tall, lean form framed by the darkening sky at his back.

He surveyed the place where she lay like an invalid, and his eyebrows met in a scowl. Stepping in, he closed the door behind him and then turned toward her, gesturing with the crutches. "What is it? What's happened?"

"I had an accident."

"Obviously." He set the crutches down at the foot of the couch and began stripping the leather gloves from his hands. "Tell me about it."

Kate looked down at her lap, unconscious that her fingers were pulling at the threads of her skirt. "I had a bad fall."

"When?"

"Sunday, after you left."

Sam lifted his head. "I see."

Succinctly, she explained what had happened. When she stopped speaking, there was another long pause. Then he unzipped his jacket. She noticed that he was wearing a heavy ribbed sweater beneath it, and gray cords. He looked great.

"Is it my fault that it happened?"

Some of the emotion bubbling inside Kate turned into annoyance. Why did everyone want to take the blame?

"It's no one's fault. It was just an accident."

He didn't look as if he believed that. "All right, if you say so. But tell me something else. Does this mean you're through with competition for a while?"

"Permanently." Her voice was crisp. "I'll be too old to start again next year, and my brother is going to find another partner."

Sam raked a hand through his thick hair. There was a guarded expression in his eyes. "How do you feel about that?"

In her opinion there were far more important issues than skating to be discussed, and she stole a faintly resentful glance at him. Sighing, she pulled herself up against the pillow at her back. "Right now I'm not feeling very good about anything. Missing the Easterns is the least of it."

Still he wasn't satisfied. "Does that mean you're not too disappointed? Be honest with me."

"I've always been honest with you. I never wanted to be a competitor." Of course, she'd just realized that wasn't strictly true, but she wasn't going to say anything more about it. The competition was now a thing of the past.

Sam continued to study her in silence. She kept her head bent and didn't look directly at him. But she was well aware of him standing there. What did he want, she wondered. Had he come to tell her that he and Carol Langford were back together? Swallowing, she steeled herself to take the news without flinching.

"There was a message at my office that you'd called," he finally said.

She looked up at him. "Is that why you're here?"

"No. I would have come, anyway."

Kate wove her fingers together and held on as if they were an anchor in a stormy sea. "When I called the *Globe*, they told me you were in New York."

She could actually feel him stiffen and go on the alert. "Yes, I was."

"Are you here to tell me why you went?" It was agony to force out these questions, but somehow she managed to do it in surprisingly measured tones.

"Yes," he answered. "I went up to see Carol."

Ice seemed to move down Kate's spine. "That's what I thought."

Sam made an abrupt motion with his hand. "I can see what's on your mind," he grated. "But you're wrong. You've been wrong from the start." In the next moment he was sitting beside her on the edge of the couch. With gentle but determined pressure he pulled her fingers apart and enclosed her cold hands in his warm ones. "Kate, I'm in love with you. Surely you must know that."

"What?" She goggled at him.

He continued to imprison her hands tightly in his. "I think I've been in love with you almost from the first. I was afraid to admit it to myself or to you. Love hadn't treated me very well. I'd been burned, and for a while there it really did seem like the old cliché about jumping from the frying pan into the fire."

"What about Carol Langford?" she asked in a faint voice.

He leaned forward and spoke earnestly. "I should have told you about her. I've admitted that. But at first it didn't seem important. And then later..."

"Yes?"

His blue gaze met hers without faltering. "Later I guess I was afraid you'd have the kind of reaction you did have when you found out."

"But you went to see her."

"Yes." He straightened, but his eyes never wavered for an instant. "I needed to be absolutely sure that I was being square with you. I went up to talk to her and to find out exactly what my feelings toward her are now. Kate, it's over between Carol and me. She's going in her own direction, and I'm going in mine."

Kate felt a wild impulse to lock her arms around his neck and never let go. Could what he was saying really be true? She had to be sure—it was too important not to be certain!

Sam was watching her anxiously, waiting for her reaction as if his life depended on it. But she didn't look directly at him. Instead she once more lowered her gaze on her small hands, which still rested in his big ones.

"Sam," she began in a smothered voice. "There's something I have to tell you. I think you might be wrong about Carol. I don't believe she left you because of her ambition. She doesn't seem like that kind of person. I think it's more likely that she gave you up because she thought that would be the best thing for you. So you see, she was really being generous."

"Because of the difference in our ages, you mean."

Startled by the dispassionate tone of his voice, Kate looked up. "Yes."

"You could be right."

"What?" Now she really was surprised.

Sam was still gazing at her earnestly. "I've done a lot of thinking about what happened. Kate, you have to understand something. When I moved to Baltimore six years ago, I felt cut off from my friends and family, and I was a real lonely guy. Carol was lonely too, and we helped each other. But there came a point when we both began to realize that it wasn't going to go on working." He shook his head. "Who knows? Maybe that's why I brought up the marriage issue. Subconsciously I must have known she wouldn't go for it."

Kate stared. As Sam talked, she was beginning to see his affair with Carol Langford from a different angle. It was, as he'd insisted earlier, more complicated than she'd realized. "Do you mean you were really ready to break with her?"

Sam struggled for the right answer. This time he wanted to be absolutely honest with Kate. He wanted her to understand how it had been with him.

"I was ready in one way, but not in another. It was a wrench, and when she left, I was lonely again. Then I met you." He held up a hand. "I know what you've been imagining. But, Kate, I swear I wasn't using you. I was falling in love with you. You knocked me flat from the beginning, but I kept thinking, what if it's just on the rebound? Or what if I let myself go nuts over this girl, and it turns out she'd rather have a skating career?"

"But you know now that the skating isn't important to me."

"I know it if you tell me it isn't."

"Then consider yourself told." Kate cocked her head. A warm feeling was beginning to grow inside her, but after all the misery she'd been through, it seemed too good to be true, and she wasn't yet ready to acknowledge it.

"What about the rebound part of that?" she asked cautiously. "Do you still think that whatever it is you feel for me might just be on the rebound?"

"God, no!" Despite her efforts to hold herself stiffly, he hauled her into his arms. "What I think now," he insisted gruffly against the top of her silky head, "is that I'm crazy about you and scared to death of losing you. I've been going nuts these past two weeks. Kate, tell me that you forgive me, and that it's all right between us again."

Part of her longed to say the words, but somehow she still couldn't. "Carol might be still in love with you."

He sighed and then pulled back a few inches. "While I was up there, we talked about it. She loves her job, and she's found someone else, a television ad executive a few years older than herself. They've started living together, and they're talking about getting married."

Kate felt as if a great weight had been lifted from her shoulders. "And what's your reaction to that? Do you feel jealous?"

A flicker of annoyance darkened Sam's blue gaze. "Why can't I make you understand? I'm in love with you and not with anybody else. There will always be some feelings between Carol and me, but it's not what you seem to be imagining."

"I have a very good imagination," Kate agreed. For the first time in the course of their conversation, a smile began to lurk at the corners of her mouth.

Instantly Sam picked up the slight change in her mood and pulled her close to his chest again. "What does it take to make you believe me?" he demanded fiercely.

His hands were on her arms, and as she glanced down she suddenly caught the costly glint of gold at his wrist. She stared at it, and Sam, following the direction of her fixed gaze, guessed the reason.

"Did Carol give that chain to you?"

"Yes, it was a Christmas present." Without hesitation, his strong fingers went to the chain and snapped it. Then he took Kate's hand, dropped the glittering links into her palm and curled her fingers tightly over them. "Take it, Kate, and keep it."

Her mouth framed an "oh" but no sound escaped her.

"Keep it as a pledge," he continued. "Carol's found someone else, and I'm glad, because so have I."

She held the broken chain tightly in her fist and exhaled a deep, shuddering breath. "You really think that you're in love with me?" she managed to whisper. Just saying the words was a pleasure. It gave her an even greater thrill to hear Sam's fervent response.

"I don't think it, I know it. And you feel the same way about me. Admit it."

He tipped her face up so that she was compelled to meet his gaze. Looking directly into his eyes and watching them darken to indigo, she said, "I fell in love with you from the moment I saw you, and I think I'll love you all my life."

EPILOGUE

CHRISTMAS LIGHTS twinkled from the enormous tree dominating Kate's tiny living room. She and Sam had spent the latter part of the afternoon decorating it. Now that it was dark outside, they sprawled comfortably on the floor in front of the glowing pine, a bottle of wine between them and the remains of the picnic dinner Sam had brought.

"Will it hurt your leg if I put my head in your lap?" he inquired.

Kate brushed some bread crumbs from her skirt and smoothed out a place invitingly. "Not at all. My knee stopped hurting days ago."

He nodded and then made himself comfortable. When his dark head was cradled in her lap, he looked up at her through the shadows. "You're a remarkably fast healer, Ms Coleman. You were off those crutches in no time, and now you're hardly limping at all. Maybe you really could be back on the ice in time for the Easterns."

Kate shook her head emphatically. "Not a chance. I'm not interested. And besides, Chris has already found himself a new partner that he's gaga over. I wouldn't interfere with that for anything."

Sam couldn't keep the pleased expression from his face, and when she saw it, Kate matched it with a smile of her own. Twirling a strand of his dark hair between her fingers, she looked down into his face and thought about how much she loved him. She'd been so happy these past few days that it almost hurt.

"You know that hill overlooking Ellicott City, the one you can see from the window by the bookcase?" he asked unexpectedly.

She nodded.

"Well, there's a house for sale up there. I've made an appointment to see it Monday. Do you think you might be willing to go with me and take a look?"

Kate's breath caught in her throat. "I thought you liked living in Baltimore."

"I do. But I think I might like it out here better." Gently he seized her fingers and twined them with his. "Will you come?"

"Of course."

Once again his smile was satisfied. "Good. Now how about our presents? It's Christmas Eve. Let's open them."

"Don't you want to wait until later?"

"No." He sat up and gave her trim waist a squeeze. "Let's open them now. You first." Scrambling forward with boyish eagerness, he retrieved a small box from under the tree and placed it in Kate's hand.

When she saw its shape, her eyes widened. Sam had arrived that afternoon with a bagful of wrapped gifts and put them under the tree so quickly that she hadn't had time to examine them. But now as she began to undo the ribbon, her fingers trembled on the silvery paper. They shook even more when she uncovered the square velvet box inside.

"Oh, Sam," she breathed when she opened it and stared down at the diamond ring nestled inside.

"I love you and I want to spend my whole life with you," he said huskily. "Will you marry me, Kate?"

Her answer was quick and unequivocal. "Yes." Then they were in each other's arms, kissing hungrily, their arms wrapped tightly around each other as though they never intended to let go. His mouth still on hers, Sam slowly lowered her to the floor. Her hands had already begun to tunnel under his sweater, wanting to feel his warm flesh. Now his hands, as well, sought intimate contact with her body. It was as if they needed to seal the bargain they'd just struck with a physical union that would make it real.

Pulling her silk blouse free of her waistband, Sam found her breast and stroked the quivering flesh until Kate moaned with pleasure.

"Are you sure your knee doesn't hurt?" he whispered against her lips.

"I'm certain."

"Good." His voice was deep with meaning. "I've been going crazy with wanting you. Oh, Kate, you're all I've ever wanted in a woman, and if you'll give yourself to me, I swear I'll make you happy."

"I'm already so happy I feel as if I'm going to burst," she murmured as she touched the smooth velvet of his back. "There's only one thing you could do to make me happier."

"What?" Sam asked, his eyes a deep, deep blue. One of his hands was gently sliding up the warm, sensitive silk of her thigh.

Kate's golden eyes glimmered up at him, and she said huskily, "I think you already know."

MUCH LATER, as Kate and Sam lay in each other's arms, content and utterly satisfied, she suddenly reared her head and looked accusingly up into his face. "You haven't opened my present."

"What?"

"You're not the only one who has a present to give."

After disentangling herself from him and shrugging on her blouse, Kate selected a large, gaily wrapped package from beneath the tree and presented it to him ceremoniously.

Sam chuckled. "Santa Claus was never like this," he said, eyeing her dishabille approvingly. Then he unwrapped the gift and lifted the lid from its white cardboard box. When he saw what was inside, he raised an eyebrow.

"Figure skates?"

Kate nodded, watching his reaction closely. "You are going to dance with me, aren't you?"

He turned toward her and took her in his arms. "Anytime, anyplace. From now on, lady, you've got a partner."

Harlequin Temptation

COMING NEXT MONTH

#97 HEAD OVER HEELS Leigh Roberts

Monk Brown's arrival turned Phoebe's quiet
boarding house into a three-ring circus . . . and
her life into a sensually charged adventure.

**#98 STRAIGHT FROM THE HEART
Barbara Delinsky**

Heather Cole's interest in Robert McRae was
strictly medical—till he distracted her with his
wonderful bedside manner. . . .

#99 A FACE IN THE CROWD Shirley Larson

Five years ago their eyes had met across a concert
stage. Now Toni had to contend with
Cay Sinclair, the famous but reclusive rock
singer, in the flesh.

**#100 SOMETHING TO TREASURE
Rita Clay Estrada**

Sparks flew when Leo, a devil-may-care
playboy, met up with Brenda, a struggling,
divorced mother of three. (Last book in a
trilogy).

What the press says about Harlequin romance fiction...

"When it comes to romantic novels...
Harlequin is the indisputable king."
— *New York Times*

"...always with an upbeat, happy ending."
— *San Francisco Chronicle*

"Women have come to trust these
stories about contemporary people,
set in exciting foreign places."
— *Best Sellers*, New York

"The most popular reading matter of
American women today."
— *Detroit News*

"...a work of art."
— *Globe & Mail*, Toronto

WORLDWIDE LIBRARY IS YOUR TICKET TO ROMANCE, ADVENTURE AND EXCITEMENT

Experience it all in these big, bold Bestsellers— Yours exclusively from WORLDWIDE LIBRARY WHILE QUANTITIES LAST

To receive these Bestsellers, complete the order form, detach an
send together with your check or money order (include 75¢ postag
and handling), payable to WORLDWIDE LIBRARY, to:

Quant.	Title	Price
_____	WILD CONCERTO, Anne Mather	$2.95
_____	A VIOLATION, Charlotte Lamb	$3.50
_____	SECRETS, Sheila Holland	$3.50
_____	SWEET MEMORIES, LaVyrle Spencer	$3.50
_____	FLORA, Anne Weale	$3.50
_____	SUMMER'S AWAKENING, Anne Weale	$3.50
_____	FINGER PRINTS, Barbara Delinsky	$3.50
_____	DREAMWEAVER, Felicia Gallant/Rebecca Flanders	$3.50
_____	EYE OF THE STORM, Maura Seger	$3.50
_____	HIDDEN IN THE FLAME, Anne Mather	$3.50
_____	ECHO OF THUNDER, Maura Seger	$3.95
_____	DREAM OF DARKNESS, Jocelyn Haley	$3.95

	YOUR ORDER TOTAL	$_____
	New York residents add appropriate sales tax	$_____
	Postage and Handling	$___.7
	I enclose	$_____

NAME _____

ADDRESS _____ APT.# _____

CITY _____

STATE/PROV. _____ ZIP/POSTAL CODE ____

WW-1-3